Hurrah to Annamarie Jagose. Her first novel is a delight.
Tantalisingly and sensuously, *In Translation* unfolds a story that
peels back the layers of time, experiences, people and text to
reveal a polished surface rich in narrative detail.
—Simon Garrett *Dominion*

ANNAMARIE JAGOSE was born in 1965 in Ashburton. She
returned to New Zealand in 2003 after more than a decade living
and working in Melbourne, and is currently Associate Professor in
the Film, Television and Media Studies department at the University
of Auckland. She is a guest at this year's Auckland Writers and
Readers Festival.

She is the author of three novels; *In Translation, Lulu* and *Slow
Water*. *In Translation* won the PEN Society of Authors Best First
Fiction prize in 1994. Her most recent novel *Slow Water* won the
Deutz Medal for Fiction in the Montana New Zealand Book Awards
2004. It also won the prestigious Australian prize, the Victorian
Premier's Literary Award for Fiction in 2004 and was also shortlisted
for Australia's premier literary prize, the Australian Miles Franklin
Literary Award.

T0159766

in translation

annamarie jagose

victoria university press

VICTORIA UNIVERSITY PRESS
Victoria University of Wellington
PO Box 600 Wellington
www.vuw.ac.nz/vup

© Annamarie Jagose 1994

ISBN 0 86473 275 9

First published 1994
Reprinted 2005

The author gratefully acknowledges the
assistance of a Todd Foundation New Writers' Bursary.
Previous drafts of parts of this work have
appeared in *Sport* and *Meanjin*.

National Library of New Zealand Cataloguing-in-Publication Data
Jagose, Annamarie.
In translation / Annamarie Jagose.
ISBN 0-86473-275-9
I. Title.
NZ823.2—dc 22

Printed by Printlink, Wellington

If the past is to be read as present, it is
a curious present that we know to be past in
relation to a future we know to be already in
place, already in wait for us to reach it.

Peter Brooks, *Reading for the Plot*

I

Five flights up from the business of the yard, from the children's games of cricket, the car washers, the mattress plumpers, from the chicken and firework sellers, from the watchman's radio and the sweeping of the houseboy, I find a quiet comfort in these few rooms. A study, a bedroom, a bathroom, a kitchen. The walls are white, the floor tiles blue-grey. Sometimes, as I walk from room to room, not wanting to be in one room more or less than another but simply to be in motion, my feet moving through sunlight, fans turning overhead, the word *serenely* comes to mind. My world has shrunk to this manageable size, to these whitewashed walls and cool stone floors, this bounded view of the courtyard below and the street beyond. The thin curtains move in and out of the open windows. Pigeons choke on the window ledge.

Across the road at the end of the lane, the last fruit and vegetables of the day are still displayed for sale, lemons and limes, bananas, pineapples, a handcart of grapes. That time has passed when everything here was only a reminder of something more real somewhere else, when a word here completed a sentence begun in that other country, when two, five, twelve times a day, the faces of strangers briefly converged with those other faces which I had abandoned, which had abandoned me. Yet still these small reluctant fruit, which from my apartment window are barely smears of colour, remind me inevitably of another garden and the possibility, daily diminishing, of a more promising harvest.

My days revolve about this desk, a felt-topped card table with the green fur worn down to the wood at one corner. I have my routine here, my timetable. Every three days or thereabouts, I pick up from the post office the latest instalment of Nishimura's novel. Every third day I forward the previous page of work. I imagine those cool blue envelopes making my journey in reverse, travelling along Marine Drive, past Haji Ali's tomb to the Santa Cruz airport, a touchdown in Singapore, then to New Zealand, to Wellington, the curves of the bays, Oriental Parade, Courtenay Place, Taranaki, Vivian, Victoria and Aro Streets, the slow climb of Raroa Road and finally the dark slot of that letterbox whose photograph I have before me as I write, Navaz on this side, me on that, on the morning of our departure, staring down the barrel of a time-release Nikon, knowing already from Lillian's example that the function of the camera is not to record but to frame.

I arrived a stranger in that city I now think of, from this distance, as home. I came by rail from one of those country towns not big enough, yet not quite small enough, to overlook impropriety, with the hot breath of scandal fresh about my head. I took up my space on the arrivals platform tentatively, like the opening chapter of a novel, feeling myself to be the origin of who knows what lost or seized opportunities, who knows what unimaginable events, what coincidences and calamities, what quickenings of the heart and blood, and even as I stood there before the baggage car, the ether swirling with my unknown future, I felt the delicate tug of some narrative in the making fastening itself securely, double clove hitch, at my ankle.

There seems little point in moving on, in taking up the twin weight of my story and my suitcase, in drifting to the main entrance with the other passengers whose unawareness that they are bit players in my story lends their performances a convincing naivety, to the taxis and the Raroa Road address written out in my mother's girlish hand, if you are derailed by the word *scandal* and must lie, wheels turning in the air, until its precise shadings are calibrated. Telling your story is never a simple matter of possessing a glittering eye and stopping one of three. I will not distort my story's natural line, pushing it off centre, swelling it here and there with premature disclosure. Scandal will out, as my mother said at the time, complacently altering popular wisdom for her own narrow purpose.

I arrived, then, in the city with the hot breath of scandal fresh on my skin. At home, such a sulphuric breath set me apart, and eventually drove me, from the milkily sweet smelling herd. The city, though, is full of smells. The city is a smell. Every brick or stone of the city, every blade of grass, leaks a smell which accounts for its specificity in the city's history and, mingling with all the other smells, provides an account of the city itself. Here, the smell of countless feet, of dust and exhaust fumes, is stabilised by the insistent tartness of dog piss and the last traces of an unspeakable loneliness. Here, the daytime smell of the park, the easy sweat and sun lotion, is pierced through by the darker tang of secret and stolen couplings, of solitary indulgences, poverties of pocket and spirit. And in the democratic city where smells, like shift workers, are continually taking the place of others, what point is there in distinguishing between, even less, what possibility of cataloguing and ranking, smells? The nose whose olfactory powers might specify all the smells in the city's bouquet, might separate the smell of fear from the smell of money, the last whiff of an old crime of the flesh from the wet ash smell of dead hope, has yet to be born. Scandal is only one, and not even the worst, of the smells of the city.

My taxi nosed away from the stand and, like a horse given its head, bore me through the city streets to a hill suburb overlooking the harbour, to a letterbox whose inscription matched exactly those words my mother had written down for me and pressed into my hand in the place of any other more obvious gesture of farewell. *E.R. Morrow* and beneath this another line *51 Raroa Road*. My aunt was standing in the window at the front of the house while I paid the driver. She was still standing there, centred in the glass and flanked on either side by a statuette of the Virgin Mary with stars at her feet and its companion piece, a dumpy-faced Baby Jesus in crown and cape, as I shut the cab door and crossed the pavement. She did not look pleased to see me but not, in all honesty, displeased either. She looked as if she had been waiting there since breakfast.

The path stretches to infinity as my aunt's scrutiny dollies before me, tracking, in close up and slow mo, my approach to her house. I unleash a smile in her direction, which catches awkwardly at the corners of my mouth, twisting one higher than the other. I turn, put my case down and latch the gate. I feel suddenly European, black and white, laden down by the significance of my smallest gesture, like a character in one of those late night Saturday Playhouse films that

I would stay up for at home, alone, the only human consciousness for miles, my family sleeping about me in the darkened house. My aunt's beetle eyes graze the back of my neck.

As if viewing myself from a distance, I see the slouch of my shoulders, see myself as my aunt must see me, head down, latching her gate, her sister's daughter, cowed, and coming to her in disgrace. I turn, lift my case, grown suddenly heavy, and walk into her stare as one walks into a head wind. Inside the frame of my aunt's insistent surveillance, my head moves abjectly up and down like a horse's, each step carries me closer to her stinting generosity. It occurs to me that my aunt has no idea of the circumstances of my shift, that my mother would have represented my trajectory as not a falling away from shameful disclosure but the first step in a promising career in city banking. I square my shoulders accordingly. I swing my suitcase. The advantage shifts so that she, on the eve of her travels abroad, must stand apprehensively in her own home as I, the young banker, someone with prospects, swing carelessly down her path to take her place. I savour for a moment the brief impression of her face, a pale moon seen through glass, before I mount her front porch with an almost jaunty step.

I arrange myself expansively in front of the door, hands in pockets, elbows thrown wide, legs straddling my suitcase. A minute passes, then another. My ready smile exhausts itself. After a foolish hesitation, I ring the doorbell. My aunt appears almost immediately.

'Helena,' she cries, extravagantly pronouncing it *Aylayna*, 'how you have grown.' Her liberties with my name, along with her claims of my increase, reduce me efficiently. I feel myself shrivel like an old balloon as I lurch across her threshold.

My aunt shares a smell with her house, a mustiness of old carpet and thighs clenched shut for too long. It is difficult to say whether over the years the smell she manufactured had leeched into her French polished surfaces, the thick fall of her drapes, the seal on the S-bend under her kitchen sink, or whether, like a piece of cheese in a refrigerator, her body has become encoded with the smells surrounding her. Falling asleep that night, I listen through the wall to my aunt's quiet, almost furtive, preparations for departure. That smell infiltrating my nostrils, the unresisting pillow giving back into my ear the regular sound of my own breathing, I am snatched from sleep by the sudden image of my aunt tenderly cradling my cheek against the cool flaccidness of her belly.

Now, in this room over the courtyard, fans turning, it is cool thoughts of another belly, a ribcage, the line of hair on an upper lip, the cleft of an armpit, that bend me over my papers, that shuttle me between two languages as, pen in cauliflower hand, I work to translate myself into another country, another tongue, another story.

2

How much depends upon a chance meeting, an invitation, a closed or open door.

One morning at my aunt's house, I cleared the letterbox to find a surprisingly formal note from Lillian and Navaz, my aunt's next door neighbours. The honour would be entirely theirs, it said, if I would attend their 'little party' that night. They had seen me several times, and had intended to call on me long before, but a peculiar combination of circumstances had prevented it—signed Lillian and Navaz, in one elaborate hand. I wore my black jeans, a loose silk shirt of my aunt's tucked into a heavy buckled belt and, a little after seven, I stepped through the hedge separating my aunt's garden from theirs.

A group of people are standing on the front porch, smoking. I can hear their voices, although not what they are saying; their cigarette tips glow and fade. Someone gives a hooting laugh. I press around the side of the house making for the back door. A couple are arguing in the kitchen; I hear them through a window, open above my head. It is a tired script for two voices, worn through in places with repetition.

'You said we could go home whenever I liked.' The man's voice is high and petulant.

'But we've only just arrived. When I said we'd only stay as long as you liked, I didn't mean leaving as soon as we got here.'

'You said we could go home whenever I liked.' His words are drunkenly, precisely, separated from each other.

'Give it half an hour at least.' She takes a conciliatory tone. Underneath the window, I can almost read her parenthetical stage directions.

'I didn't know *he'd* be here. Why do they invite him and his dirty . . .' The last word is indistinct. I'm not sure whether it is 'tricks' or 'trick'.

'You're shickered, dear.' She is coolly diagnostic. 'You know what you're like when you're shickered.'

I open the door. He is sitting at the kitchen table, head in his arms. He looks up, they both look up as if glad of the distraction, when I come in. She leans against the opposite wall, her cocktail matches the green of her sheath dress. His hair is dark, receding, and he wears, like me, dark trousers and a loose white shirt.

'First time?' she asks.

There is the sound of glass breaking from the front room, more laughter, and then someone is hurrying down the corridor towards the kitchen.

'Helena,' says this woman in a way that suggests *at last* rather than *is it?* 'Lillian.' She takes me by the elbow. 'So glad you could make it.' Lillian is tall and thin and there is something not quite right about her face, a tendency to separate out into its constituent parts, like a composite picture used in police identification.

Lillian steers me out of the kitchen and halfway down the hall where she leans me against the wall like an ironing board. In the open front door, a woman with a ballet teacher's cheekbones and tightly pulled back hair is nodding energetically at a much shorter man. Each abrupt jerk of her head seems to pull another phrase from between his lips. Lillian leans over me confidingly.

'We watch you sometimes in your front room,' she says, confessing that indiscretion so lightly an intimacy is presumed between us. 'Oh you are patient, I have seen you sit hours, where something might have floated up.'

This is how Lillian talks, as if quoting something. Always, this is how I will remember her. Her words have, for me, a familiar, half remembered quality. They hold themselves apart from other speech, from the tedious argument begun again in the kitchen, from the telegraphic utterances of the man in the doorway, the murmur of voices from the front room, as if, having passed through Lillian's lips, they are forever quarantined in quotation marks. Even her clothes are a citation. She is dressed in the classic sportswear look of the 1930s. In a calf-length straight skirt, fagoted silk blouse under a soft sweater and a close fitting cloche, she is Faye Dunaway in *Bonnie and Clyde*. She has a mouth that troubles you when you first meet her, and troubles you more later.

Lillian takes me by the elbow again, guides me into the front room. Here, sitting on the couch and armchairs, on cushions on the floor, standing backs to the fireplace or, through the open French doors, against the porch railing, eating, laughing and smoking, putting down glasses too heavily on the mantelpiece and floor, are what my mother would only describe as 'a crowd'. For my mother, 'a crowd' is a contemptuous term, a qualitative, not a quantitative, description, justified less by the number of persons gathered in one place than their perceived moral slackness, their turpitude. Lillian leads me around the room, not introducing me to anyone but giving brief accounts of them like a guide in a museum. The three men in tweedy jackets are poets, 'dear addicted artists', who write sonnets to each other and declaim them in tequila bars downtown. The woman eating canapés, her flesh the colour of an elastoplast, claims a connection to the Hungarian royal family. The doctor's wife is having an affair with his receptionist. Of the Spanish maid she says nothing. And the maid, as if she knows there is nothing to be said, moves about, filling a glass, offering a napkin, without saying a word. Her remoteness is a study in superiority, not deference.

Lillian describes her guests with a viciousness that is not unflattering to herself. She leans back against the wall, head close to mine. The amusement which narrows her eyes does not extend to that troublesome mouth. The whole party has been just for this moment, an unspoken complicity which swells my heart against my ribs. Then Lillian is gone, I am alone, and must take a seat in a room full of strangers. At the end of the couch a woman mimes to the song being played on the stereo. Her lips move in perfect time. *There goes my heart again*, she mouths, *There goes my heart again*. I judiciously estimate the amount of couch to place between myself and her, not so little that we are mistaken for friends, not so much that anyone—one of the poets, for example—feels obliged, or even able, to talk to me. The cuckolded doctor is fishing for an olive at the bottom of his glass. My *chanteuse* smiles politely at me between tracks. *I don't want to set the world on fire*, her lips are moving again, she holds up her hands on either side of her face, fingers flickering in an imitation of flames. *I just want to start a flame in your heart*, she sways back and forth, one hand tapping out a heartbeat over her left breast.

I am already planning my escape, calculating whether it would be less obtrusive to slip away past those smoking on the verandah or cross the room and leave by the front door, when Lillian appears in the doorway with the maid. They stand there together, talking, every now and then one or other of them looking across the room to where I sit on the couch. The maid picks her way towards me.

'Something to drink?'

I shake my head.

'Something to eat?' She points her chin at the table where the Hungarian princess is still grazing on the canapés but I am a resolute Persephone, determined not to impede my departure from this other world.

'This is an unusual party for me. I've met Lillian but I haven't even seen Navaz. I live over there,' I wave my hand at the invisible hedge in the distance, 'and they sent over an invitation.'

For a moment she looks at me as if she fails to understand.

'I'm Navaz,' she says suddenly, correcting my pronunciation.

Then I am hurrying towards the door, Navaz at my side. It is difficult to say whether I am making a dignified exit or being shown off the property. Lillian is there and laughing at my confusion.

'Come over tomorrow when all these others have gone,' she says as if my presence alone is enjoyed and the rest are some crude horde, swilling and smoking uninvited. 'Around eleven.'

Later that night, hearing voices carrying in the dark, car doors slamming, laughter, I get up and cross the damp lawn to stand in the gap in the hedge. The last few people are leaving, saying *goodnight goodnight* and *thank you* on the front steps. The party is over. I am as dark as a tree trunk and can see into the front room, lit up and seemingly bigger now empty. I wait for Lillian and Navaz. They return in a few minutes; Navaz paces the floor as if measuring it for new carpet. I wait for that revelation, my midnight devotion rewarded, some sign, perhaps a kiss I think giddily, some Strauss on the stereo, but Lillian and Navaz come and go, as if unwatched, picking up a glass here, straightening a rug there, until Navaz pauses a moment in the doorway, turns off the light and is gone. I wait in the dark until all the lights are out before returning to my own illuminated space, my room, my sleeping mat.

3

At lunch, Lillian and Navaz talk about themselves for my benefit. They describe their work. This is how they refer to it, *my work*. Navaz is a translator. Lillian is an artist. I am glad that my lips, a little greasy with quail, do not have to form the words *bank teller* at that table. Thin bones wreath our plates. Navaz lights a cigarette. There is an interlude, a break in proceedings, as if all the talk of lunch has been a curtain-raiser for some more significant encounter. My hand around the stem of my wine glass seems alien to me, a strangely thin paw I have not seen before. Lillian asks, as if continuing rather than initiating a discussion, 'And so how did you come to our city, Helena?' Two pairs of eyes and a burning cigarette end are trained on me.

I do not know where to start, every possible beginning seemingly disqualified by a previous event, exchange or aspiration that necessitated my exile from home and family. The monkey's paw lies upturned on the table in front of me. Even when I limit myself to a chronology of events, reminding myself of those lists rote learnt for history class, *Five Causes of the First World War*, no beginning obviously asserts itself. I think of my return to the laboratory storeroom, no longer a schoolgirl yet so recently elevated from this status that the bells and uniforms now function for me as the erotic signs of an authority that might be exceeded. How naked the science teacher seemed surrounded by the almost transparent flesh of blunt-headed dog fetuses suspended in formaldehyde. I do not think of her frightened and tearful, recanting before the disciplinary board, preferring to remember her spread out, like a frog on the dissecting table, my face in the warm folds of her neck. I think of my unloosing that first button, the gap between the two front teeth—*incisors are for cutting, girls, molars are for grinding*—in which I insert my tongue but only once, the sensation of tongue on gum reminding me unpleasantly of the dentist's, my silent exertions since I cannot bring myself to say 'Mrs O'Malley' nor allow myself, as I do alone at night, to call her 'Eunice'. Like Lolita, she has one name at school, another in the seizures of love.

I am ashamed to tell any of this to Navaz and Lillian, not for the reasons my mother used in an attempt to inculcate shame in me—*a married woman, your old teacher, no bed or anything*—but because it does not seem sufficient. Our plates are stacked one on the other, our glasses are refilled. I need a story substantial enough, nuanced enough, to bear the weight of my gratitude for this meal, the afternoon sun only now angling onto the kitchen table, for Lillian and Navaz watching me in my aunt's front room, for their being translators and artists. I remember such a story, a case history I read once, far more elegant than mine, involving a beautiful and clever girl of eighteen, an older and more worldly society lady and parents, a forceful father, a neurotic mother, who were not only scandalised by, but implicated in, their daughter's infatuation. This was the story I chose to tell, my splicing of the two narratives less a lie than a gift.

'When I was eighteen,' I began, 'I became devoted to a certain woman ten years older than myself. My parents insisted that, although she came from a good family, this woman was nothing but a *cocotte*.'

I amused myself by attributing this word to my parents, who would doubtless be as unfamiliar with such a foreign tag as with a society lady of questionable morals.

'My parents said everyone in town knew that Eunice lived with a friend, a married woman, and had intimate relations with her while nevertheless continuing promiscuous affairs with a number of men. I did not doubt, indeed I hoped, that these accounts were true and I seized every opportunity, however slight, to be with Eunice, to ascertain all her habits, to wait for her for hours at her bus-stop or outside her house, to send her gifts of flowers.'

I took a pleasure in this simple repetition of Eunice's name which I had never been able to use previously and felt a sudden pang of regret that I had never given her flowers or any kind of present.

'One day while walking with Eunice, I met my father not far

from his office. He cast a furious glance at the two of us, having come by that time to know of Eunice's reputation and my fondness for her. When Eunice asked if I knew the man who had given us such an angry look, I confessed that it was my father who had absolutely forbidden me any connection with her. I hoped that such a confession might raise between us the topic of our relationship, that we might at least talk about that which, until then, had consisted in little more than a few embraces and kisses.'

Telling this story was easier than I had hoped. I felt slightly estranged from myself as eighteen, clever, wilful, passionate, and my voice had the synthetic modulation of a skilful orator. Nevertheless, I was making the story mine in a way that exceeded my assumption of the subject position, the case history was coming back to me in chunks, *nothing but a* cocotte, *intimate relations, girlish pleasures*. Lillian and Navaz also seemed familiar with the story. They nodded in recognition when my father made his furious discovery, showing a close attention only when I elaborated on or deviated from the original. They exchanged a glance when it was revealed that the *cocotte*'s name was Eunice. That they had also read this case history and knew that it was no more my story than theirs was no embarrassment to me. Far from feeling caught out in a lie, this produced in me a determination to present Lillian and Navaz, at their table, with the most beautiful rendition of our shared story.

'I had hoped to force from Eunice some sympathetic declaration but instead she was angry with me for incurring my father's displeasure. She ordered me to leave her then and there, and never again to wait for her or to address her. The affair must now come to an end. I felt a curious jab of pleasure. Eunice had described my attentions, and her own far more casual reciprocations, as constituting an "affair", yet only to declare that affair over, having run its course. I rushed away, yet I cannot say I was wholly despairing, and flung myself over a wall down the side of a cutting onto a suburban railway line which ran close by.'

I gave a small and rueful smile, remembering the ordinariness of that narrow-gauge track, the oil-stained stones between the rails, a piece of paper blowing across the siding.

'I spent a considerable time recovering in bed, although fortunately little permanent damage was done. When I was able to get up again, I found it easier to get my own way with my parents, who no longer opposed me with such determination, and even Eunice, flattered by my plunge on to the railway tracks, treated me more warmly than before.'

Smoke from Navaz's cigarette curled in the sunlight above our heads. I imagined myself, freshly armoured with a sickroom frailty, forcing tenderness from my parents.

'After about six months of this, my parents became worried at my renunciation of educational studies and girlish pleasures. They confided in the family doctor and it was recommended that I should see a specialist.

'A *Jew*,' my mother whispered to me before my first session, as though this were some impressive qualification or accomplishment. His rooms, in an office block, were filled with books and aboriginal artifacts, a feather and bone head-dress. We discussed the effects on me of my first sighting of my younger brother's genitals. He explained that my mother's recent pregnancy had upset me since I wanted my father's baby for myself. To punish my father for his disloyalty I had withdrawn my affections from men entirely, becoming masculine myself and taking my mother, in my father's place, as the object of my love.'

Lillian and Navaz accepted these accounts of my feminine and masculine identifications blandly, their nodding heads marked time like metronomes.

I was fast running into trouble. While able to insert myself into the story in various ways, marking it as an autobiographical account rather than a medical case history, there was increasingly a pressure from the patient faces of Lillian and Navaz to dovetail this story with an explanation of my arrival in the city. There was the untold story of awkward backroom fumblings, a schoolgirl crush made grotesquely comic in its fleshly realisation, and my exile from home; then there was this elegant tale of adolescent passion and vain parental sanction. The two ran parallel—like the railway tracks on which I had so histrionically flung myself—with no hope of convergence. It occurs to me now, my doctored version of the most recent instalment of Nishimura's novel still wound on to the typewriter in front of me, that much of my adult life might be explained in terms of my attempts to appropriate some narrative or other. Like the cuckoo's egg, I am always finding myself in a strange nest, hoping that the rightful occupants will mistake me for their own.

'The doctor explained that I was impervious to his treatment because I transferred to him the sweeping repudiation of men which had dominated me since I suffered such a disappointment at my father's hands. He said that I distanced myself from the important insights his analysis uncovered, as though I were a *grande dame* being taken over a museum and glancing through her lorgnon at objects to which she was completely indifferent. He broke off the treatment, then, and recommended to my parents that they continue, but with a lady doctor.'

My story wound down lamely. It was getting late.

'My parents were interested in following his suggestion but I refused further treatment saying instead that I would not see Eunice again. The prospect of life without her was so bleak that, just as once before I threw myself on the railway tracks to avoid such misery, now I bought a train ticket and, crossing that same stretch of line again, made the night journey down to the city.'

I finished my story, which I realised too late was probably more of a performance piece than suited a kitchen table, to a silence taut with applause withheld.

'So, that is how you came to our city,' Navaz said, smiling across the table at Lillian who was smiling at me. 'By train.'

4

By its very nature, memory, like desire, is incomplete.

The city, which had initially seemed to me a source of inexhaustible possibility, stretching out on either side of the taxi windows, soon rearranged itself less generously as a strongbox, advertising its riches through the very act of withholding them. My aunt took her leave with the minutest of farewells. I began my work at the bank. Every night, every weekend, and later and more desperately, every morning before work, I flung myself at the city, abandoning myself to its ravishments and befoulings. I gave myself up totally to the slow turning wheels of that sordid machine. Repeatedly I threw myself into the brinish tumult whose slipstreams and undertows were familiar to me from De Quincey, Proust and Colette; repeatedly, I was thrown back on dry land, untarnished, untouched. Like the victim who must, in the end, open his eyes, now clenched deliciously against a blow that never falls, I came to learn that the city was less interested in scorching its mark on my uninitiated skin than I was in bearing its brand.

With the reversed instincts of a spawning salmon, I would plunge downhill from my aunt's house, bent on destruction. I smoked hashish with a visiting professor of economics, lying on a mat at the back of his cousin's shop. I dressed as Marlon Brando in *The Wild One* and, eyed by sailors and stevedores, had my hair clipped at the barber's on the wharf. I walked the night streets, climbing the stairs to a doorway's yellow rectangle of light whenever I heard music and voices conspiring above my head. Whatever was given me, I ate, drank or smoked, once downing in a single gulp a shot of tequila and a raw oyster without ever knowing who in that crowded bar had sent it my way. I moonlighted as assistant to a bald tattooist, swabbing down strange flesh in the intimate closeness of his parlour. I moved through that dirt and those promises of enslavement like a saint among lepers, surrounded by a corrupt worldliness which could not be persuaded to feed on me. The early hours of the morning found me walking slowly home, tired but inviolate. The city was letting me slip through its sieve as dispassionately as, a few hours later at the bank, I would count out hundred-dollar bills, touching each one with a moistened fingertip, insensitive to its value or power.

I moved through the city's underworld like some cursed Pollyanna, turning every crude brutality into a thing of whimsy and charm. My very appearance in some after-hours bar or low dive ensured a certain theatrical cast to the place. Beside me, thugs were unconvincingly thuggish, over-scarred and tattooed; in my presence, illicit transactions became indistinct from acts of legitimate business. Like the effete choreography of gang fights in *West Side Story*, I could empty a scene of menace. It became more and more difficult to imagine myself in a state of depravity or even dereliction. For one thing, there was my dependable job and regular income. For another, there was my aunt's house with its cruet sets and antimacassars, its pantry stuffed with home preserves and the coy sign on the toilet door, *'Tis here*.

My aunt writes to me from Australia. Rather, she sends me a photograph of herself in a lemon angora jersey, the Sydney Opera House a white flare behind her. Her thin shoulders almost manage to crowd the opera house out of the picture. Her chin is raised, her eyes glitter. She looks angrily across the Tasman or perhaps that is just the angle of the sun. There is a message on the back: *E.R. Morrow, Sydney*.

I no longer hurried home after work to change into boy's clothes and buy drinks for sailors. I turned my furious attention on my aunt's house. I boxed up the holy water dispenser, the curlicued candelabra, the photographs, gilt framed, of my parents proudly displaying their children like prize marrows, of my aunt's former pupils on their wedding days, the coconut wood trinkets from her years in the Pacific, the fat face Baby Jesus pointing dolefully at his exposed and bleeding heart, the sheet music and the runner from the top of the piano. I hid from sight the dozen birthday cards from the mantelpiece, the tapestry cushion cover of a woman in a blue dress with a unicorn resting its horned head in her lap, the Cardinal Wolsey bowl, the decorative platter in eight Australian hardwoods. At first I simply planned on ridding myself of daily contact with the banal detritus of my aunt's existence, the flabby domesticity that made a mockery of my banishment to the city.

These objects were stored out of sight in the garage, yet the release I sought still plainly eluded me. I ceased merely clearing surfaces and began gutting my aunt's house in earnest. I emptied the book shelves, took down the light fittings and the curtains, rolled up the rugs. When the garage could not accommodate another wall hanging or fireguard, I began emptying the front of the house into the back, the living room into the kitchen, the main bedroom into the spare one, the corridor into the bathroom and toilet. The television in its heavy oak cabinet stood against the stove. The single bed in which I had fallen asleep, listening to myself breathe on that first night, lay upturned, legs in the air, on the double bed. The couch, two armchairs, a scotch chest, the bedside table, an anglepoise lamp, the bookcase, the drinks cabinet: all were dragged from their rightful places and set adrift in the back rooms. When the last piece of furniture, a difficult double wardrobe, was wedged into the bathtub, I closed the door at the end of the hall and never opened it again.

Counting the hall, I now had three rooms in which to live. The front door opened directly onto the corridor which ran down the middle of the house, what had been the living room on the left, the bedroom on the right. I say 'what had been' as if the former régime, with its self-satisfied pairing of domestic space and human function, could be escaped so easily, as if the exiled furniture did not constantly assert its solid hulking presence through the closed door at the end of the hall. For the next few days, I moved around the front rooms as though the furniture I had struggled to shift was not missing but merely invisible, a delusion I was assisted in by the many imprints of table, chair and bed legs, bookshelf bases and lamp stands, that continued to pock the carpet, its pile flattened by a phantom weight.

This ghostly afterlife of my aunt's furniture made me more uncomfortable in the house than the total absence of any of the convenience associated with a domestic life. With no means of storing or cooking food, I took to having a large meal downtown during my lunch break. While the other tellers ate a pot of yoghurt in the park or read magazines standing in the newsagents at the corner, I was sitting down in a hotel restaurant to tomato soup, roast lamb, potatoes, peas, carrots, pumpkin and lemon meringue pie. This meal, which I took like a pill, was my unchanging diet for the next eleven weeks, interrupted eventually, and most spectacularly, by Lillian's brunch of deep-fried quail marinated in *mirin* and *nam pla* with wild rice pancakes. While I dined midday at an inner-city hotel, I whiled away my evenings at the public library, always washing myself surreptitiously in the toilets before leaving for the night.

It was during one of these visits to the library that I found a solution to what I increasingly thought of as the problem with my living arrangements. I was reading my way through the periodical stands as one might sift for evidence, thoroughly, ignoring nothing, however slight. The periodicals were arranged alphabetically and it had taken me slightly under a fortnight to read *Airlock*, the aviation industry's union magazine, the *Alexandrian*, a journal of philosophy, and *Amaranth*, the newsletter for a botanical appreciation society, when I came across *Architecture: International Forum*.

There, in an article entitled 'Zen Precepts in Californian Precincts', a Japanese architect, Yoshio Taeko, described the process of transforming his client's conventional bungalow into 'a meditative retreat that does not struggle against the city but provides a point for its contemplative observation'. I did not spend much time on Taeko's essay. It was nailed down in places with phrases like 'Eastern serenity', and 'a modern lifestyle'. It concluded: 'One does not inhabit a house, a house inhabits you'. No, it was the photographs of Taeko's work, rather than his statements of design philosophy, that caught my eye.

Even given the distracting, frequently foregrounded presence of Taeko's client, one meat-faced businessman, Teddy Morgan, the photographs convey an undeniable sense of proportion and tranquil purpose. A simple courtyard of sand raked around a boulder had been created in the middle of the house. All of the rooms, pale wood floors, chalk walls, were arranged about the courtyard, poised between this inward view and the outward sweep to the city. Here Teddy hunkers awkwardly by his bed, a thin mattress laid directly on the floor; here he stands at an outside facing window, in an attitude of contemplative observation, inexplicably cradling to his chest a blue porcelain bowl. I check the magazine out of the library and walk the long way home.

My aunt writes to me from Singapore. This time she is photographed standing beside a five-and-a-half-foot mannequin of Colonel Sanders outside a Kentucky Fried Chicken shop on Orchard Road. She does not partake in any of those sillinesses people imagine they invent when being photographed with mannequins. She is not laughing, or smiling even; she does not mimic the Colonel's puffy plastic features. She has one protective arm about his shoulders and she leans into him, close, as if attending to some softly worded complaint. The message on the back of the photograph reads *E.R. Morrow, Singapore.*

For the next three nights, I study the photographs of Taeko's work as if they were maps of a dangerous country I am soon to pass through. I become more familiar with Teddy's body than that of my father, which is beginning already to fade alarmingly from my memory. I can only remember my father piecemeal, the stretch of his shin above his sock, the hair of his nostril, his thickly creased palm. Teddy's body, however, becomes achingly familiar to me. (Why does that phrase ask to be guaranteed by another, 'as familiar to me as my own'? Who do we think inhabits their body so easily, with such a familiarity, that they encounter mirrors or photographs without a jolt of pleasure or disgust?) Certainly, I know by heart the backs of Teddy's huge hands as they clasp that bowl but also, and equally, I know the hidden palms and wrists with their tracery of veins. I memorise the powerful thighs and square face from the sleeping mat photograph but there can be no surprises for me in the unseen stretch of suit fabric across shoulders and buttocks, the twin crown at the back of Teddy's head. I can see that, despite a certain enviable bravado, Teddy is frightened and misses his bungalow.

That weekend I take up the carpets and find, like a favourable portent, blond wood below. I strip the walls of paper and paint them white, washing over them with a pale blue in an impulsive homage to Teddy's porcelain bowl. Using the money from the sale of the carpets, I hire a commercial sander, strip back and then varnish the floors, one room at a time. From a gymnasium supplies store, I buy a tumbling mat and place it in the left-hand room which, lacking the one necessary piece of furniture, I realise, slightly self-consciously, I cannot refer to as 'the bedroom'. In a borrowed trailer, I haul a load of clean, dry sand from Scorching Bay and, removing the only statuesque stone from the municipal rockery, recreate Taeko's courtyard garden, complete with rake marks, in the centre of the right-hand room. The house is perfect. I sit before the rock and sand as if before a television. I sleep like a baby on the mat.

The only thing out of place in my rooms is the red and black cover of *Architecture: International Forum*. I return it to the library the next night. Remember that cover's Spanish kitchen, its red formica sweep, its bone-black stone floors, the copper pots shining over the bench. Although I remove it from my house, having finished with it, it has not finished with me. Even now, it is lying in wait, thousands of miles away, on a low table in Professor Mody's apartment, anticipating already the unimaginable sequence of events that will carry me from this island to that subcontinent, from this city to that, predicting the kaleidoscopic substitutions, reversals and abandonments that will lead me to a certain door, a certain narrow staircase, an armchair only feet away from the low table on which it presently, and patiently, lies. This is the first coincidence.

5

The second coincidence is my aunt's postcard which arrives in the mail the next day. She has made the postcard herself by putting a stamp on the back of a photograph. This is the least picturesque of my aunt's communications. My aunt stands on a street corner before a shop front, a grocery store or perhaps a pharmacy. Everything seems a little flat in the harsh glare of the sun. She is wearing a pair of very dark wraparound sunglasses which have the appearance of a black blindfold. The condemned woman waits against the shop window. Above her head, a man stands, as if in judgement, on the verandah of the flat above the shop. He is wearing a fawn safari suit. He is Professor Mody, retired reader in Japanese Literature. My aunt's handwriting on the reverse is less informative than usual. *E.R. Morrow* it says, *Kemp's Corner.* I have no idea what city this might be. If it were not for the stamp, I would have no idea what country.

The days pass. Split in two, they are structured by different ordering systems. At the bank, an order is imposed by the columns of credit and debit, the running tallies, the decimal point's precise punctuation. Each morning I unlock my cashbox and keep careful account of every incoming or outgoing. Each night my day's transactions must concur with the original float. *Float* seems the perfect word for this sum which, released from its anchorage, spends its day adrift, buoyed up on a tide of other figures. At home, order is no more lightly enforced by a lack of regulation, by vast tracts of time in which it is only possible to progress, neither fast nor slow, downstream to the next day and the opening of the cashbox. Now, when I keep myself together by working late into the night at this green-felted card table, I wonder that boredom did not gnaw at me during those solitary empty evenings. I cannot say how it was, only that each evening spent by my sand and rock installation seemed too full for boredom, *so perfect is our inoccupation that boredom becomes impossible.*

Fancying myself to have withdrawn from the city, I resented the smallest intrusion on my seclusion. Sometimes during those evenings as I sat or lay on the polished boards, wondering when, and how, my life would begin in earnest, the telephone would ring. Muffled in the darkness of the barricaded kitchen, its ringing sliced through my rooms. I did not need to answer the telephone to be connected to another scene which I thought I had escaped, the living room at home, my parents sitting, stolidly as bookends, on the couch, my mother, a freshly made cup of tea at her side, muting the television and saying to the side of my father's head, as if unawed by the possibilities of long distance, 'I just might give Helena a call.'

My aunt's postcards continue to arrive. Their sequence through the letterbox suggests an impossible itinerary. Shortly after the photograph of Kemp's Corner, a postcard arrives from Italy. My aunt is holding a string bag of fruit in one hand—tomatoes, grapes and perhaps apples—and in the other, a large loaf of flatbread. She looks very upright in comparison to the Tower of Pisa, tilting in the background. The caption on the back is resolute: *E.R. Morrow, Italy*, it says in handwriting angled like the tower. In the next photograph my aunt is standing by a swimming pool, her face silvered by waves of light reflected off the surface of the water. In racing togs, my aunt is as bony as a fish. A certain vanity allows her to place one hand on hip. The back of the card reads *E.R. Morrow, Hotel Happiness, Austria*. A week later, another card arrives. My aunt is sitting on a road marker at the edge of a field. Behind her a man in a straw hat is herding geese. *E.R .Morrow, Bali*. There is no longer any congruence, or even logical relation, between the photographs and the stamps. The poolside picture from Austria carries a Greek stamp and postmark, although no photograph ever arrives from Greece. The Italian card is franked at the Gowalia Tank Post Office in Bombay, a place I imagined my aunt to have left weeks ago.

I arrange these pictures of my aunt, stoutly turning her back on the great sights of the world, along the mantelpiece. There is a satisfaction to be had in this frieze, in which, in shot after shot, my aunt's diminutive frame dwarfs the great monuments to civilization. My aunt seems neither exhilarated nor discomforted by the foreign.

She places herself in front of it, inserts herself between it and the camera. Her lemon knitwear, her collarbones, her picnic lunches intercede for the strange. She is not, I think, a tourist at all. Tourists, after all, can be divided into two groups and, being tourists, can move from one group to another as the mood takes them. There are those who move themselves from place to place for the thrill such dislocation affords. They write to friends 'back home'—a phrase they use, not with fondness, but pity—detailing all they have seen and eaten. Back in their own countries, they hear each other's confessions, 'Every now and then I get the travel bug and simply have to take myself off,' pretending a ruefulness over that which they hold most dear. There are those who travel insulating themselves as much as possible from the experience of movement. They recognise each other in hotel foyers and on bus tours, clucking and shaking like fowl. 'Not a square of toilet paper in the whole place,' they might say with a shiver of pleasure, or more triumphantly, 'And not a one of them speaks English.' They scour the globe, driving themselves through customs barriers and across time zones, to reassure themselves of the superiority of that piece of the world called 'home'. Tourists are engineers of a collision between their bodies and the exotic. My aunt, however, has a certainty about her that isolates her from her surroundings. She is not alienated, but distinct, from those strange scenes that fall behind her like pantomime backdrops. She is always, and without doubt, 'my aunt', uninflected by foreign language and unfamiliar vegetation.

Looking down on to the courtyard from my fifth-floor window, I fantasise my aunt's appearance at the bottom of the lane. Although a stranger here, her blue stare and purposeful tread make the inhabitants of the yard seem out of place. She walks awkwardly, limping against the weight of her suitcase, her blouse sticking damply to her chest in the heat. A group of children furrow behind her, thin arms across each other's shoulders. Their voices pipe in a schoolroom English. *Good morning. Which country are you from?* They run at her, their arms, thin as wickets, spinning in a fast bowl. *Excuse me please. Do you know King Hadlee?* She does not stop to ask directions and I lose sight of her as she walks past the watchman, into the entrance hall below. How impervious she would be to the yammer of two, or is it three, unknown tongues filtering up from the yard, to the elusive authority of the Japanese/English dictionary always open on my desk, its sly offering of one word for another. I imagine her taking my place at the card table, as once I took hers, her unchanging sense of herself—*E.R. Morrow*—easily filling these few rooms. I imagine her dispatching my day's translation in the half hour before breakfast, scarcely pausing where I have spent uncertain hours adjudicating between 'maid' or 'hired help', between hair as black as a 'crow's' or a 'raven's' wing. She would work for thirty minutes, perhaps forty-five on a difficult day, before making a start on her real business, placing herself between the camera and the yellow basalt arch of the Gateway to India, before Hutatma Chowk which everyone still only knows as Flora Fountain, before the old woman's shoe in the Hanging Gardens.

I am much more timid about inserting myself into this city's frame. When I leave the apartment I always have a destination in mind and, like a train bound to follow its tracks however the road might diverge, my route to each place is unvaried. A right turn at the end of the lane and through the traffic lights about half a mile in the direction of the hospital takes me to the Gowalia Tank Post Office where I clear Navaz's postbox and buy airmail envelopes. A left turn, then a downhill swerve past the park takes me to Kamal's and a paper *masala dosa* for dinner. The bank is across the road at the end of the lane, between the padlock shop and a grocery where I sometimes buy a cold Thums Up or a Chocobar. I tame the city by superimposing on its seething streets, its unimaginable cul de sacs and short cuts, another map, the simple trajectories of my excursions, blue for the bank, green for the restaurant, red for the post office.

This standardisation of my forays into the dizzying world beyond the lane does not prevent, but lessens the possibility of, the city bringing its cruel weight to bear on me, squeezing the bones in my skull and bubbling the blood in my veins. One day on my way to the post office, yesterday's airmail envelope in my shirt pocket, I step around an encampment of road menders, looking away from where a labourer suckles her child against a mound of shingle, and catch sight of myself in a shop window, a grocery store or perhaps a pharmacy. Coming across my pale face unexpectedly surprises even me. I have lost weight. Lillian's cotton shirt hangs on me like an unconvincing disguise. Something shifts inside me, some memory stirs itself, and the scene arranges itself more familiarly about me, this shop front, this unforgiving light, this overhanging verandah. Dimly reflected in the glass above my shoulder, the world continues to play itself out behind me, pickaxes rise and fall, a double-decker bus moves slowly past the road workers. I am in my aunt's postcard. The door to the upstairs flat is closed. Its brass plate announces *Professor Mody, Retired Reader in Japanese Literature*. I ring Professor Mody's bell, hear first its chimes dissect the unknown space beyond the door, then the shuffling step of the retired professor on the stair.

6

Listening to the slow feet on the staircase behind the closed door, I have time to study myself distorted in the uneven surface of Professor Mody's brass nameplate. His name and position scar my forehead, dark whorls break up the surface of my face. There is some scraping of metal, a jangling of chain, on the far side of the door, which now opens, slowly, inwards. For a moment, in the gap of the opened door, I see Professor Mody as he was in my aunt's photograph, in a khaki safari suit, beak-nosed, with that erect posture that suggests deportment classes or back injury. Then, as if he has been expecting me, he turns and ascends the stairs, leaving me to close the door and follow him, pulling my shirt free from my belt, combing my hair back with nervous fingers.

The staircase is narrow and, as I follow a step or two behind Professor Mody, I watch the button-down flaps on the back of his suit, as if they were the rungs of a ladder I am climbing. The stairs end in one bare room, larger than my four run together. The harsh light of the street is filtered through the white paper blinds that hang at every window; a fountain plays against the back wall, the splintering noise of stones being broken almost forgotten in the fall of water in its marble basin. Professor Mody glides across the stone floor as if on castors, indicating the armchair where I am to sit. He remains standing, tracking back and forth behind the low table in front of me. He talks in a soft voice which I barely hear. Slung in this chair, my knees at the same level as my ears, I am remembering Nandalore and the first auto-rickshaw ride Navaz and I ever took, our feet up on our suitcases in the cramped compartment.

I register the strained tones of an inquiry repeated and look up at the professor who has ceased his pacings to stand, eyebrows up, forehead creased, before me.

'You have brought your work with you?' asks Professor Mody, his voice, like his eyebrows, raised in question. I fumble in my crouched position for the blue airmail envelope in my pocket and place it, face down, on the table. Professor Mody looks at it—it is obviously sealed—he looks at me. Yet I, who without compunction intercept Navaz's mail, steaming it open over a saucepan of water on the gas ring, seem suddenly unable to open this envelope again for the professor. I tell myself, then, that my reluctance arises from the fact that Nishimura's envelope is already dangerously weakened and will only sustain one more opening but, more than that, it is because I feel that its typewritten contents are a private communication from me to Navaz. I would as soon show these pages to a stranger as I would a note in my own hand beginning *My dearest Navaz*.

The professor is waiting for me to explain myself; I feel incapable of such explanation. Three minutes ago I was on my way to the post office, picking my path around a pile of dusty rubble in the hot city street. Now I am sitting in front of a man known only to me through a photograph and a nameplate, my letter between us like an untranslatable cipher. And next to the letter, on the same low table, is a magazine whose familiar cover is another shock for me but for which you, at least, have been prepared. A curve of copper pots hanging from the ceiling, the red and black of the Spanish kitchen: it is, of course, *Architecture: International Forum* and I know, without looking, that the piece of paper I can see marking the professor's place is inserted at the first page of Taeko's article.

And it does not end there, this ridiculous piling up of coincidences, the hallmark of heavy-handed fiction, this plunging from now to then which renders the present nothing more than a series of unstable trapdoors over a more memorable past. For now Professor Mody is speaking again, his voice once more soft with reassurance.

'It does not matter,' he says, and at first I cannot remember in what exactly I have disappointed him.

'It is your first day only. I will fetch us something to drink and you, you will give me three words please.' He places a piece of paper before me, a pen is handed over.

'Three words please,' he repeats at the door and is gone. The fountain continues to play, the paper blinds move in and out on the waves of heat coming off the street, first tapping against the window sills, then billowing slightly into the room, scoring laser lines of white light on the dark stone floor. I am, as they say, miles away, months away, banking over the countryside surrounding Nandalore, the aeroplane's shadow like a cartoon on the red dirt landing strip below.

The airport at Nandalore is dusty and dry. At the edge of the tarmac one dog mounts another, its skin gleaming in pale patches through its fur. The mounted dog does not look up from where it is grazing the hot stubbled grass like a cow. I watch Navaz as we wait for our luggage to be unloaded from the plane: her nose hooks over her mouth, her hair shines as if oiled. She is beautiful, so beautiful I cannot bear her to look at me. Once again I have her to myself, I have cut her away from her family, leaving only her outline behind. Outside the terminal, in the early morning sun, a line of auto-rickshaws are waiting. We climb into the first one with our suitcases and direct the driver to Hotel Printravel. There are no doors on the auto-rickshaw and the sun warms our legs. Our feet are up on our luggage and we hunch to each side, trying to see where we are. A tree, a country road: we could be anywhere. The driver steers around a goat. Navaz squeezes my leg above the knee, gives me that small smile. On the road up ahead another rickshaw is stopped. The drivers call to each other and our driver climbs down to help the other change his tyre.

'Please read this,' he says, passing an exercise book over to the back seat. 'I will be a moment only.'

Navaz and I bend our heads diligently over the book like studious pupils, as if we think the driver will examine us on it when he returns. We look at each other enquiringly as we near the end of each page and turn to the next with a wet finger. Each entry is in a different hand and each extols the excellence of Prakash as a guide to the town and the surrounding caves. *For a very reasonable rate Prakash showed myself and my wife about his town. My wife instructs me to write that Mr Prakash is a real gentleman.* Some of the authors are ambivalent in their address, urging the other tourists who will surely follow them to make full use of such an opportunity *to see the real India* and praising Prakash himself who is certain to read what has been written as soon as they are out of sight. *Prakash is the most genuine Indian we have met in the last three weeks*, writes one, *Please look us up if you are ever in Adelaide.* At the back, as an appendix, there is a collection of postcards sent to Prakash from Switzerland, New Zealand, Nepal, Spain. *Dear Prakash, Got home safely. We were talking about you the other night at dinner and we remembered how you liked to collect postcards from your satisfied customers. Good luck for the New Year.*

Prakash is back at the rickshaw, wiping his hands on an oily cloth.

'I am Prakash,' he says, unnecessarily though ponderously, as if he is the heroine in a Victorian novel, mistaken for a girl of low birth, whose declaration happily clears a path for a good marriage. I have not really seen Prakash before, only the back of his sleek head as he sits in the driver's seat. He is short but muscled, like a tiny weightlifter; his eyes are dark and the sleek lick of hair that falls across his forehead reminds me of a seal cub.

'Perhaps you two ladies would like to put my talents to the test?' He himself seems unconvinced by such a line and busies himself with the cloth, polishing each of his hands in turn.

'I am a real gentleman,' he says, quoting the couple from Manchester, and starts the rickshaw with a jerk that throws Navaz and me against each other in the back seat.

On the way into town, Prakash talks to us, shouting over his shoulder against the noise of the two-stroke engine.

'You are from Australia?' he shouts. 'I have many Australians.' The rickshaw bounces along the road, its toy wheels catch against the stones and throw up spurts of dust. Navaz and I heave up and down in the back.

'In six years, I have taught myself English,' says Prakash. 'Now I will learn Japanese. My friends all teach me when I show them around. You will give me three words please.'

He looks over into the back seat where Navaz and I are jiggling from side to side.

'Three words please,' he repeats. 'Three English words.' Suddenly I do not know a single English word. I look at Navaz whose brain is full of words, English, Japanese, German, Russian, and those little switchpoints that turn one word into another. She is looking out the side of the rickshaw at a chicken, the thinnest chicken I have ever seen, rolling in the dust at the side of the road.

'Chicken,' I say foolishly, gripping Prakash's shoulder with one hand, pointing behind us with the other, as if the word itself is not enough, to where the chicken continues to thrash on the ground.

'*Chicken* I already know,' says Prakash dismissively, showing his teeth white against the brown of his face.

Nobody says a word: the only sound is the chainsaw buzz of the rickshaw's engine. I look out my side of the rickshaw at the scenery scrolling past. I am sure, without turning my head, that Navaz is allowing herself a small smile at the thought of my 'chicken'. There are fields of some leafy crop stretching back from the road, every now and then a woman is working, a roll of cloth twisted about her head, there are small buildings with smoke winding out of the roof. Here, and again there, a 'chicken' stands mockingly, scratching the ground with its scaly feet, throwing dust over its outstretched wings. We sail down the road, jibbing from side to side, the countryside behind us joining together again at our wake as if we had never passed this way. I stare and stare but the world is suddenly, for me, unspeakable. The neat captions that once labelled everything, that we exchange with each other, are no longer available. What is that green crop called, whose star-shaped leaf is unfamiliar to me? Are those little buildings 'houses' or 'kilns'? What is the name of the women's headgear? Nobody says a word: the rickshaw passes between the fields, pulling them together on either side like a dusty zip.

'Tarmac,' says Navaz. I turn to look at her. She *is* smiling slightly, lightly, in her fashion.

'Tar-mac?' asks Prakash, screwing himself around in his seat to face Navaz. His neat parting cleaves his head in two like an axe blow. Over his shoulder I watch the road as if I am the driver.

'Tar-mac.'

'It is the surface the plane lands on,' says Navaz. Prakash nods complacently, as if the definition is less valuable than the word, as if he always knew where the plane landed but not the 'tarmac'.

'Pneumatic tyre,' says Navaz.

'*Tyre* I already know,' says Prakash. 'New-magic?'

'Pneumatic,' says Navaz, 'A tyre inflated with air.'

Prakash drives with a new seriousness. *Pneumatic, tarmac,* he makes these words his own.

We are on the outskirts of town. The fields have given way to buildings recognisable as houses, and a garage, with two Hindustan Ambassadors parked nose to nose on the forecourt, now passes by the side of the rickshaw. A weight of expectation rests heavily on the third word, as in fairy tales it rests heavily on the third dream, the third wish, the third son. Navaz is still looking out her side of the rickshaw at two boys sitting high on roped-together bamboo scaffolding, painting a billboard advertisement for butter. I try to think of a word that Prakash will not know. *Kursaal, plumassier, rowel.*

'Shorts,' I hear myself say. Navaz does not turn her head.

'Shorts,' repeats Prakash, without much pleasure.

'They are like trousers but they finish here.' I make an amputative slicing gesture across my own thighs. Prakash is turning in his seat to see my demonstration.

'I know the thing,' he says now, with some excitement. 'Shorts.'

And then here is the Hotel Printravel, its name in faded blue lettering over the door. Navaz and I climb down. Prakash arranges our suitcases on the pavement beside us, one on each side, as if he is about to take our photograph. We stand there stiffly while he climbs back into the rickshaw.

'Get cleaned up,' he says. 'Have a rest. I will be back at nine-thirty to take you on tour. One hundred and twenty rupees for the day, the best deal in town.' Navaz and I have not discussed Prakash's offer to guide us around Nandalore but we nod anyway, our murmurs of gratitude lost to the engine's roar.

We are shown up to our room on the third floor. It is a large white room with three single beds arranged in a row like a school infirmary. Tattered mosquito nets are drawn around each bed. There is a bathroom with toilet and shower, a balcony overlooking the street. Down below a group of schoolboys are being walked in pairs by their teacher. They wear tiny blue blazers and their blue caps have visors which overhang their faces like beaks. Watching them and their little, careful steps, I am reminded again of my 'chicken' and my face flushes hot. Navaz is in the bathroom, turning on the taps to the shower, in accordance with Prakash's instructions.

'There's no hot water,' she calls, after a while. Our urge to travel, to move from place to place and 'see things', seems already to have exhausted itself. We have come to rest like a pair of bullets that never reached their target. We are tired, dusty, don't know our way around and there is no hot water. I stand by Navaz who is sitting, naked, on the toilet. Even like this, she is beautiful. When she first took off her clothes for me, I drew the curtains and would not let her turn on the light. I wrench the hot tap uselessly one way and then the other.

'I'll go downstairs and ask,' I say.

Downstairs, I explain that there is no hot water in our room. The man behind the desk is wearing a blue jacket and looks like a grown-up version of those schoolboys I have just seen being herded along the street. I wonder if he is also wearing 'shorts'.

'You must ring the bell in your room,' he says reproachfully. 'A boy will bring you buckets of hot water.'

I climb the stairs again. It is nearly nine. Navaz is lying on one of the beds, under the mosquito net, like a leftover piece of cake. I ring the bell and five minutes later the same man from reception, not in shorts at all but a pair of white cricket trousers, knocks at the door.

'Yes?' he asks blandly, as if we had never spoken.

Professor Mody returns carrying two tall glasses and a jug of something cool, clinking with ice, on a tray. I am as he left me, doubled up in my chair, the sheet of paper blank on the table in front of me. At last, he is reproving. He holds the tray higher than is necessary and away from me, as if to punish me by withholding its pleasure.

'You have done nothing,' he scolds. 'I have been squeezing lemons for you, and for me, there is nothing.' I am sorry to disappoint this man, with his straight back and squared shoulders, who has invited me into his home and made me lemonade.

'I didn't know what words you wanted,' I say now, my excuse weak in my own ears.

'But on the telephone,' says the professor, still refusing to put down the tray, 'You said you understood my instructions. You said you would bring your work. But you bring nothing.' The tray is put down not because Professor Mody has finished but so that he can point at the sheet of paper lying on the table where he left it.

'You do nothing.' There is no need for pointing. The paper lies whitely between us.

'I have never spoken to you on the phone.' At least I can explain something. 'I only saw your picture once and today I saw your nameplate on the door.'

'You are not Miss Betty, then?' asks the professor, my name, like his line, reinstalling us within that overwritten melodrama we seem unable to escape.

I shake my head. The professor's hand rises to his throat in fear.

7

I think of myself infrequently these days. There is no mirror here, no ritualised, domesticated exchange of words and glances, to give myself back to myself. I am in suspension, not simply hanging over the yard and its noisy, immeasurable transactions, but in suspense, an alertness to what lies ahead deadening me to my surroundings. Like those bodies on ice in Californian crypts, whose suspended animation is underwritten by science's pledge to discover a cure for the diseases that would have killed them had they not first consented to this temporary and refrigerated departure from the living, I wait, my past a series of imprints on my cerebellum, my future a deferred promise, my present a chill blank. I wait. Until these last months, I did not know myself to be possessed of such a capacity for patience. All my work, my visits to Professor Mody, my collections and dispatches at the post office, my mornings of dilemma over 'a crow' or 'a raven', over 'a maid' or 'hired help', are less concerned with doing than deferring. They facilitate my waiting. I have assembled about myself a life that, like scaffolding, is a structural support but temporary.

My real life is conducting itself elsewhere. It continues without me, marked by my absence, like those painted showground tableaux of faceless musclemen and women in bikinis whose circular holes, through which you might insert your own face, are a necessary and untroublesome breach in the scenario's surface. Meanwhile, my daily existence is driven by the twin pistons of memory and desire. Even now, when a hundred times a day I fantasise a letter from Navaz, a phone call, her return, our wordless reconciliation, when her absence here is cold ash in my mouth, I still wake unprotected, the night watchman clearing his throat and spitting, the pigeons gurgling on the sill, and look across the pillow to that blank space, that white sheet, where Navaz once was and is no longer. I know how she would be lying there, what shape she would make under the sheet, what warm smell would rise from her as she slept, pillows pushed aside, face directly on the mattress. She haunts me, marks me, as once long ago, shortly after I arrived in the city, a time I think of now as simply *before*, my aunt's absent furniture continued to impress her carpet.

When I do think of myself it is not as someone who lives in these rooms, looks out on this view, is translating this novel, but as someone who is deficient, cloven, waiting. I compose letters to Navaz in my head in which I make declarations and give account in an economic yet delicate phrasing designed to appeal to her translator's eye and ear. Awake in the night and desperate for the ambivalent release of morning's light, I work on these letters, seldom getting further than that first troublesome address. *Dearest Navaz*, I once began a note to Navaz like that. Given her presence in the next room, the words strung across the page with an extravagant formality. *Dear Navaz, Navaz, My dear Navaz*, I try them all, the rote, the curt, the paternal address. Sometimes I abandon the problem of salutation and begin work on the first sentence. *I am still living*, but no, *I am still staying in your apartment.* I am never satisfied with the tone. *That time has passed when everything here was only a reminder of something more real somewhere else.* The first sentence returns me to the unresolved question of the address and so I fall asleep, invoking the name of one who even now, so many miles away, is getting up, smoking her first cigarette, heating the milk for the morning's coffee, without a thought for me, *My dear Navaz, Dearest Navaz, Navaz.*

I will never write to her unless she writes to me. I will never pick up the telephone and dial that long string, that final familiar clump, of numbers unless she rings me first. She was the one who said, 'I think perhaps I might go home,' those qualifiers indicating less her uncertainty than her belief in the possibility of a gentle cruelty. She intended me to go with her, of course, and I intended nothing less, yet still I punished her for her easy claim of that other place as 'home' by saying that she could do as she liked but I was staying here. She argued with me, her family were going to Matheran for the summer months, I didn't know anyone here, what would I do in the city when it heated up like an oven, I would run out of money soon, I didn't speak the language, any of the languages. I didn't say what I was thinking, *take me home, we made a mistake, I also miss Lillian*, I only repeated, do as you like but I am staying here. She was the one who kissed me, then, with those Judas lips. She was the one who left.

Navaz did not leave cruelly, exactly, but there is no such thing as a kind leavetaking. As if I were the owner of lodgings, she gave me two weeks notice. At first those fourteen days seemed like a hoard, one or two might slip past but still there were a dozen remaining, then there were only four, three, two, and these last ran out like thieves disturbed. It seemed to take a long time, that departure: there was the last visit to the Victoria and Albert Museum, the last meal with Navaz's family, the last night in bed, the last breakfast, the last kiss, the last sight of Navaz through the taxi's rear window as it pulled out of the courtyard and into the street. By my reckoning, however, a departure is never a stretch of, but a point in, time. There is all that preparation, those sad separations and packings, the bestowal of some small item of remembrance but then she is gone, and there can be no preparation for that moment, that calculable second, when you are suddenly, and unarguably, alone.

This is something I can see now, and from this distance, that Lillian got wrong in her National Gallery exhibition. This was the first of Lillian's work I saw hung: three matt cibachrome photographs, each one the size of a double bed, six foot by four. This was the first time I learned to say 'hung' of pictures in a gallery. Lillian called these three photographs *Imaginary Departures*. In the first one, *Nora's Departure*, she is wearing a long dress, navy blue with a collar mounting firmly to the chin. She has Navaz's winter coat folded over one arm, a small overnight bag in her hand. A patterned shawl, cut from an old curtain, is thrown about her shoulders. She stands in the doorway of Navaz's study, her free hand on the brass doorhandle, the strip of wall Navaz and I repapered under her instruction visible over her shoulder. In a hired suit jacket smelling of napthalene, I sit in the foreground, head in hands. All that can be seen of me is the dark triangle of my shoulder, the side of my beard, my left hand splayed over my eye. The black letters across the lintel read 'the greatest miracle of all'.

The next photograph is *Captain Oates's Departure*. Lillian is standing in the backyard against the grey concrete of the garage. She looks twice her size in a borrowed anorak, fur-lined hood enclosing her face and an outsize pair of rubberised trousers. She is wearing my beard, now grey with talcum, and her eyelashes, her beard, the fur of her hood are glistening with scrapings of ice from the freezer. A heavy snow falls across this scene. Off-camera, Navaz is blowing twelve kilograms of kitty litter out of an industrial vacuum cleaner. Lillian leans into this blast, one arm crooked across her face, the other blown back from her body, seeming to point to the orange glow of my tent pegged out behind her.

The last photograph rhymes with the first: it is *Dora's Departure*. Lillian is sitting on the edge of a doctor's couch. Her white blouse is covered in writing, one line repeated again and again: *do you know that I am here for the last time today?* It is not possible to read this whole sentence at once. A cuff might only read *the last time*, a crease at her breast makes *you know I am here*. Over the couch hangs a calendar. The date is December 31. On either side of this are two framed pictures. One is of a father leading two children from a burning house while the mother looks over her shoulder at something left behind. The other is of a girl with a travelling bag. There is a man at her side walking through dense woods past a signpost that reads, 'Two and a half hours more'. I am almost as I was in the first photograph, a foregrounded shoulder and beard.

What I know now, and didn't then, is that these photographic departures of Lillian's were less imaginary than imagined. They were only the dramatic, enactable events energised by the imminence of the departure. Small wonder then that Lillian favoured them over the thing itself for the departure is an ugly, an almost unframable, moment. If I were to recreate those three departures today, I would not need Lillian. Nora would not be standing in the doorway with her travelling clothes on. She would be gone, the downstairs door slammed shut behind her. The tent would glow unseen, Captain Oates's footprints already filled in with snow. The doctor would stare

44

in horror at his empty couch. New Year and Dora would have left already. At my desk in this strange country, I imagine Lillian's camera is still aimed at me. The only thing that survives the departure is the hunched shoulder, the head in the hands.

I was to clear Navaz's postbox every day and forward the mail to her. She had just begun translating Nishimura's latest novel which he was sending to her in airmail instalments. He had the whole thing worked out in his head, he told her once, now he was writing it down, without revision, from the first to the last word. I opened that first envelope when it arrived intending only to continue the story which Navaz used to read to me some evenings before bed, to follow the fortunes of the medical student so far from home, to trace the ever more convoluted lines of hostility and desire between the owner of the rooming house and the serving girl. Finding myself stuck on several important phrases, uncertain of whether the maid is going to the hairdresser or the hospital, I bought this dictionary from the Strand and forwarded the letter to Navaz only when I was satisfied with my own translation. This was how it began, as all these things begin, almost thoughtlessly and motivated by the simplest and most satiable desire.

It was in later weeks that my intercession in the line of communication between Nishimura and Navaz became more complicated, that my interference exceeded the twenty-four-hour delay necessary for my dictionary-assisted translation of Nishimura's latest chapter. I no longer only steamed open the blue envelope to find out whether the student was a figure of absolute ignorance or knowledge, oblivious or attuned to the soft tendrils of desire beginning to feel their way towards him across the household, or whether it was the maid or the owner who had left the book, open and underlined, on the medical student's desk.

To begin with, I only deleted the occasional phrase, as if Nishimura's story was one of those postcards given to British soldiers at the front during the first world war, from which they were allowed to erase but not to add sentences. *I am quite well I have been admitted into hospital sick wounded and am going on well and hope to be discharged soon I am being sent down to the base I have received your letter dated telegram dated parcel dated Letter follows at first opportunity I have received no letter from you lately for a long time.* Once I was familar with Nishimura's style, I began to retype his text, changing a word here, inserting a phrase there. The owner, who in Nishimura's version had *a face broad as a boat's oar* gains through my rewriting *a mouth that troubles you when you first meet him, and troubles you more later.* It is no longer a stripped down motorcycle engine, but the loamy promise of a small vegetable garden, that the medical student bends over in the dim evening light. He works until his muscles ache and then stays outside a little longer, *his back set against the lit-up front of the house.*

8

Navaz speaks five languages, can write in eight and read two more. Once when she was talking to me about a book she was reading, she asked, 'Do you have any German?' Not can you read German, can you follow it, but *do you have any*? Not having any, and suddenly feeling this as a lack, an impoverishment, I made that open handed gesture you make when approached on the street to indicate that you have come out without money, that you don't have a light. She had started out as a translator for a government department in the city but soon she was getting enough work as a translator of fiction. These were her own words: *getting enough work*. It was Lillian who showed me the shelves of books that Navaz had translated. *Against the Season*, an award-winning volume of poetry from French Canada; *Cage*, the prison notebooks of South America's most celebrated political prisoner, 'now available in English for the first time'; *The Green Fuse*, a sonnet sequence whose translation was praised by *The Times Literary Supplement* as 'maintaining the easy control, the unlabored phrasing and breadth of allusion, which marked the Russian original'.

Translation seemed to me a secretive business. I never saw Navaz actually translating anything although she spent hours at her work. She had a study at the front of the house and worked at a long desk which overlooked the garden and, beyond that, the street. Whenever I came in to see her—*to catch her at it*, was the phrase I used to myself—she would be looking out the window, a pencil tucked over one ear, dragging slowly on one of the cigarettes that were kept burning at her elbow, narrowing her eyes against the smoke. And the books themselves, their titles and authors' names running along the spine, never looked like translations. I would run my hand along their backs, take one down, open it randomly at any chapter, any page, and read the first sentences that claimed my attention. *This morning I traded my soap for a piece of paper. I have since prepared a hundred sentences in my head but none is beautiful enough to risk that smooth white perfection.* There is no sign that these words belong to someone other than that dissident whose name is displayed so prominently under the title on the front cover, that the author may not even understand the language he claims to have written. There is nothing to suggest that these lines are less real than those unseen and unintelligible ones, choked up with unpronounceable consonant clusters, from which they derive. It is only on the title pages, in the smallest typeface, that Navaz's name appears, *translated by Navaz Nicholson*, or sometimes, more specifically, *translated from the German by Navaz R. Nicholson.*

'Do you translate the titles as well?'

A small smile tightened the corners of her mouth so I knew it was the wrong question, one that would be repeated to Lillian after I had gone home for the night.

Lillian shows me a series of photographs she has taken of Navaz. When she offers to show it to me she says, 'Let me show you one of my pieces.' It is not really a series of photographs but one photograph mounted many times in the same frame. It is stacked in the back room along with Lillian's *other pieces*. In the photograph Navaz is at her desk. You can't see the desk but I recognise the blurred blocks of colour behind her as the books in her study. She is smoking, of course, a yellow pencil resting over her ear, a thick curl of smoke obscuring one eye. Perhaps Lillian has taken this shot through the glass of the front window for Navaz looks straight ahead, her single eye resting easily on the camera's. The picture is titled *Portrait of the Translator.* There is a small piece of card taped to the back of the frame with these words typed on it and underneath it states *Private Collection.* Below each picture of Navaz is a handwritten caption, a careless scrawl of dark ink which I recognise from the invitation in my aunt's letterbox, and now know to be 'artistic'. *Navaz as Milan Kundera*, says one. *Navaz as Nicole Rocquefort, Navaz as Shio Nishimura.* I am giddy with the realisation that I am standing in a *private collection*, one of Lillian's *pieces* in my hands as casually as a breakfast tray, and that I understand completely. It is the first time it has occurred to me that there might be something to understand in a picture, a way of reading that is more than just looking. I can't imagine how I might indicate this to Lillian. I stare dully at the faces of Navaz, feeling as wooden as the frame still held between my hands, Lillian watching the side of my face so intently she might be taking a light reading.

Lillian is always showing me things. It is she who shows me the dust jacket of Navaz's translation of Nishimura's third novel, *Skin Behind Bone*. Nishimura himself has written the back cover blurb: 'I always knew Navaz Nicholson to be a fine translator but her work on my latest novel far exceeds that of translation. Nicholson does not return my work to me, she rewrites it entirely. *Skin Behind Bone* is a new novel and I will say an altogether better novel than anything I have ever written. This does not debilitate me, it revitalises me. From now on, the first appearance of my work will be in Nicholson's translation.' I go to see Navaz in her study. Smoke rising, she is looking out the window. I put the copy of *Skin Behind Bone* on her desk.

'What will happen to the original of Nishimura's next novel?'

'It will come out a couple of years later as a translation.'

'But what is it a translation of?'

'Of the English text.' The corners of Navaz's mouth are tightening in that small smile. I try another line of questioning.

'What did you think when you first heard of Nishimura's intentions? What did you do when you first read this?'

'Translated it,' says Navaz.

These are the scenes I rerun for myself now, the sound of the fans turning above my head like the clacking of film from a projection box, scenes which doubtless continue, diminished, without me. Then the view from my window, the woman on the porch opposite picking over tonight's rice, the children chasing a water truck from the yard, is more remote than these grainy images from that distant country, these jerky takes of Lillian and Navaz. My memories have the hand-held quality of home movies. The camera pans across our faces, Navaz's, Lillian's, mine, swinging too close and pulling back for focus. Our lips move in silence, our unsynchronised voices trail across the next scene: *Do you translate the titles as well? Let me show you one of my pieces.* Here I am, in my aunt's white shirt, hesitating in the gap in the hedge; here we are, the three of us, lunching on the afternoon lawn, sprawled carelessly in the sun like an advertisement for sanitary protection; our faces are overexposed, bleached flat, our mouths, unfathomed holes, our movements are spastic, continuity the one thing the camera cannot preserve.

Thinking now of all that which is lost to me but to which in my mind I continually return, I remember a dream I had last night. I am at Raroa Road again, in the kitchen with Lillian. She has a pile of flour on the kitchen table and is breaking eggs, one by one, into a well in its centre. I am walking down the corridor to Navaz's study. For once she is bent over her desk, her pencil working furiously. She has another desk immediately behind her and when she finishes writing at the desk in front of the window, she turns on her revolving chair and begins working on something at the second desk. There is no pencil behind her ear, cigarettes burn on both desks. She looks up as if she has been expecting me. She says that she is trying something new, that she is translating Nishimura's novel into English, then back into Japanese, to English again. It never comes out the same. She makes the gesture of pouring water back and forth between two containers. Each time, the plot lines, the characters' interactions and outcomes, are recognisable yet recognisably different from the time before. Nishimura is pleased with her work. His publishing house is bringing it out next season as a trilogy.

This is all I ever wanted, to be moving between Lillian, breaking eggs in the kitchen, and Navaz, turning and turning in a smoky room. It is as if, too late, I realised that Lillian's photographs were the real thing, not the simulation they pretended. I live more fully in the flickering half light of recollection and dreamwork than I do in this room, in this country whose fiercely bland light allows no deception. Like some old sports hero who watches himself again and again breasting the tape, I understand that my worth is reckoned in terms of what I was once, of what used to be and, unlike that old man, I fool myself into thinking that that place waits for me still, is not lost to me with the passing of time. I wake in my narrow bed in a strange country, cast up, adrift, exiled. Below my bedroom window I see a small dot of light, glowing red, first on one side then the other, as the watchmen downstairs pass a *bidi* between them in the dark.

9

What passes between Navaz and me are these blue airmail envelopes addressed in Nishimura's hand. They rarely contain more than a single sheet of typed paper and arrive as regularly as radar blips. Every third day an envelope arrives in Navaz's postbox, thin, blue, barely capable of the hard journey. They have no urgency to them, these envelopes which arrive one after the other, but a kind of calm design, like Nishimura's prose itself, which knows already where it is headed and makes in that direction with a sure purpose. I carry these envelopes back to the apartment where, a towel wrapped around my hand, I hold them over the saucepan's steam until their glue moistens and the envelope flaps curl over like cat's tongues. I work over the typed page, when unsure consulting the dictionary, or this pocket phrasebook Professor Mody picked up for me two weeks ago at Thieves' Market.

There is an honest weight to the dictionary that the phrasebook lacks. Where the dictionary is judicious, offering one word for another, the phrasebook is aggressive and wheedling in turns. *He will not give it back to you. You need not ask him for it. He was dead yesterday.* Its sentences never coincide with those of Nishimura although occasionally, through my alterations, accommodation is made for them. *You must go and get an undertaker. He lost all his property last night.* The phrasebook has a cast of unnamed characters whose circumstances and demeanour change from line to line. *She is very poor now. Do you like to pity her? She is very sorry now.* It is difficult to imagine what straitened circumstances, what polite desperation, might compel someone to open this little book and, with an unpractised tongue, read off these lines, their pronunciations phonetically indicated below.

In this morning's envelope, the medical student is still preparing for his examinations. When he is not studying or working in the vegetable garden, he is writing home to his family, *My dearest Papa and Mama, Twelve days until my examinations. A friend of mine came up from London for the Fellowship and we discuss surgery from 8 p.m.*

till past midnight. He lives about a 15-minute walk from my place so I get good exercise into the bargain. The medical student goes downstairs to the dining room for his midday meal. He describes the food with some fastidiousness, minced beef with a sweetish smell, rice boiled for twenty minutes. Another boy says to the medical student, *Our money should buy better food than this.* The medical student shrugs. Mr Oliver, the owner, takes the head of the table; he does not eat but watches the boys eating. The maid serves more rice to the medical student. Her blouse is unbuttoned and she bends low as she dishes the rice so the medical student can see her small breasts shift inside her clothes. Mr Oliver is watching. *You are working too hard.* The maid is talking to the medical student, but she is looking at Mr Oliver. *Let me make your back.* Now Mr Oliver is on his feet, ordering the maid away, to the kitchen where dishes wait, to clear the table, to finish upstairs where beds should have been made before lunch. *I will make his back*, declares Mr Oliver, pulling the medical student to himself.

I begin retyping the page. In my rendering, the medical student, who I have called Sanki, is more philosophical, less compliant. When the other boy complains about paying too much for this food, the medical student, instead of shrugging, says *He will not give it back to you. You need not ask him for it.* I do not know what the maid and Mr Oliver are offering him; I do not know *to make a back.* I look through the dictionary, *to make a bed, make a deal, a face,* but find no solution. I will take this matter to Professor Mody tonight. He waits in every evening between seven and eight in case some such problem arises during the day. There is always some lemonade or beer; sometimes I bring salted cashews or *bhel puri* from the vendor on the corner.

When Navaz would be stuck on some word or phrase she would raise her head from her papers and, a pencil tucked over one ear, inhale heavily on a cigarette, eyes narrowed against the smoke. She would look out the window and across the garden, eyes glassy as a sailor's, fixed on something beyond the horizon, something as yet unseen. Knowing too well all the ways that I am not Navaz, I lift my head from these pages and stare over the courtyard and across the green of the gardens on the opposite hill. Here, it is impossible to be unseeing in the easy way of home. There is always something unfamiliar or inexplicable dragging at the corner of my eye. The strange evenness of the light does not allow me to forget myself. A couple of vultures circle the trees at the top of the hill, a crow screams nearby. In my mind the two connect, that distant flapping and this ugly, repeated screech, the sound of a saw on a nail. There is some other screeching in the courtyard. A woman is squatting in the dusty centre, calling up to the windows that surround her on three sides. She is selling something but I do not know what. She has a hammer and she bangs the dirt in front of her feet as she calls.

There is a moment in every day that I anticipate with a sweet urgency. It is those brief minutes suspended between dark and light, day and night, when everything is still, a breeze blows down the hill from the Hanging Gardens and then, at my window, eyes almost closed against the fading of the light, I am back in that other country. The day is over; the night, barely begun, smells of newly turned loam, of crushed sage and thyme. I am standing over my garden, muscles aching, just beyond the square of light falling from Navaz's study. It is no longer possible to see the rows of seedlings, so uniform and neat they do not yet look like plants, the thin bamboo stakes anticipating the height of February's tomatoes. Yet I continue to stand there, my back set against the lit-up front of the house, putting off that moment when I will turn and climb the stair to a bath which I can hear even now being drawn for me, to the kitchen where Lillian is grinding herbs and oil in a mortar, where the three of us will soon gather, in casual ceremony, with a bottle of wine.

When I ring Professor Mody's bell in the evenings, I hear his slippered feet descending the stair. He opens the door to me and says, 'Miss Betty. Come up.' This is the name he calls me now. He takes the newspaper cone from me, greasy in places from the hot nuts, and leads me up the staircase. Tonight we are having beer, one dark bottle between us, two glasses frosted from the deep freeze. The professor carries them in from the kitchen. In all the time I have been coming here, I have seen no more of his house than this one room, the fountain, the low table, the Japanese paper blinds. I am guessing that behind these other doors is an Indian household, perhaps even servants out back somewhere, who squeeze the lemons for my drink, pour my *bhel puri* into little dishes for the table.

'And how does Sanki do in his examinations?' asks the professor as if after a mutual friend. I flatten my piece of paper on the table.

'He has not sat them yet.' The professor sucks his breath in over his teeth. He looks like a man awaiting the birth of his first child.

'The maid and the owner want to make his back.' Professor Mody bends over Nishimura's typing.

'Yes,' he says after a while, 'we have this here too. Houses, good houses, you can go there and have your back done. It is called massage.' The professor reads the latest page from Nishimura in silence. So Mr Oliver and the maid are fighting between themselves over who gets to massage the medical student. I try to remember if we know what the medical student looks like. He has glasses because he takes them off and rubs his eyes when he is tired. I imagine him as thin and serious, with a wing of dark hair, but cannot decide whether I have made this up or whether Navaz read it to me one night before she left.

There is a real Miss Betty. She comes to Professor Mody for Japanese lessons. She is the daughter of an American couple who live in the apartments on the hill. Her father has business connections here—'He's someone big in rubber,' says Professor Mody—and her mother does good works in the city. Her parents are proud of her showing such initiative. On the telephone, her father says to Professor Mody, 'It'll all be happening in Japan in the next few years.' He calls his daughter 'my little chairman of the board.' The little chairman has no interest in the development of Japanese industry. She is in love with the son of a Japanese diplomat she met when they were both in Paris at the start of the year. Professor Mody and she translate Japanese love poetry and lately she has been bringing him her letters to check before she posts them.

'I saw Miss Betty this morning,' Professor Mody says now, putting aside the sheet of typing. 'She brings me a letter in which she writes *my bosom buzzes at your thought.*' The professor hisses with laughter. We share many jokes about Miss Betty.

10

This morning clearing the postbox, there is no letter from Nishimura but a postcard addressed to me from my aunt. The stamp, a familiar one from home, gives me almost the same jolt as the photograph. My aunt is lying on the hard tumbling mat in what used to be her living room. She is wearing a pale blouse and her skirt is pegged out on either side of her legs like a tent. She looks as though she is lying in state. Her fingers are laced across her chest, candles burn on either side of her head. Her eyes, which not even the weight of two pennies could close, stare through the camera, suspended somehow above her body, to lock with mine. A map of the world, the pink triangle of India visible at her left ear, supports her head like a pillow. The message on the back is the longest she has ever sent. *E.R. Morrow,* it says, *51 Raroa Road. Welcome Home.* I am unsure how to read the last two words. Is this an ironic staging of her own return home to a house whose denuded unfamiliarity makes it another stop in her travels to strange places? Or is my aunt addressing herself to me, reassuring me that everything is as I left it and awaits my return? My aunt, her goldfish eyes fixed unblinkingly on mine, gives nothing away.

Two things I know at least: my aunt is home again and Navaz has given her this postbox number. I imagine my aunt slipping through the hedge to the neighbour's house to see if they know of her niece's whereabouts. I imagine Lillian recognising her from the postcards I showed her, which were the inspiration for her *Travels with my Aunt* series, and inviting her in. I can see the three of them in sunwashed complicity, over a glass of wine or a cup of tea, at the kitchen table, talking about me in my absence, Navaz writing out the address which, translated into my aunt's sloping hand, tilts across the envelope I hold now in my hand. While no letter arrives from Navaz, the handing over of that address, as once, on a barely remembered railway platform, my mother handed over my aunt's address to me, is surely a gesture of farewell. At my desk, I prop the photograph of my aunt against the typewriter. It ocurrs to me suddenly that there is a touch of theatricality here—the clasped hands, the world map, the liturgical candles—which I do not recognise from my aunt's previous self-portraits. This is Lillian's work, Lillian of the fake scar and inked-in tattoo. I imagine the two of them, perhaps Navaz also, collaborating over this *piece*, my aunt arranged docilely on the mat, Lillian suspended over her, the Nikon to her eye. I reread the message as worded by Navaz. It makes no more sense than my previous readings, no more sense of the places I have left behind, of this one in which I now find myself. *Welcome Home.*

I think of the homes which I have had and which now are forever barred to me. Heading the list is my parent's house where, in my memory, it is always mid-evening, the dinner dishes have been washed and put away and a syrupy self-satisfaction falls over the four of us sitting in the living room. My brother and I—*a pigeon pair*, my mother used to say, *all we ever wanted was a pigeon pair*—are displayed like showroom models in identical armchairs. My parents sit carefully at each end of the matching couch as if on a see-saw, the upholstered distance between them seeming to place them in their proper relation to each other. It is impossible—although as a teenager, my most frequent task—to imagine them in that intimate conjunction which produced first myself and, eighteen months later, my brother. A measured hour passes in the bluish light of the television before my parents depart for bed, as if sleeping, like swimming, is not to be attempted on a full stomach. Now, I imagine my brother orbiting the couch alone. My empty armchair unbalances the room, making my parents' perch that much more precarious.

From that belljar of a house, I escaped to the city and my aunt's house where I lived, first, as a stranger, embedded in a clutter of unfamiliar objects, and then strangely, in a glossy illustration from *Architecture: International Forum.* My aunt's house slowly tightened around me like a crepe bandage. The garage was the first to slip its moorings and then the back rooms drifted from the house. I cored and halved that house like an apple. My domestic territory became smaller and smaller until one evening I locked my aunt's front door for the last time, posted her keys through the slot for letters, and crossed the hedge to Lillian and Navaz's house, where I was increasingly spending all my time and already quite at home.

I moved through that house like a canker, a tumour, and, just as the bloodstream, in fulfilling its life-sustaining task, inadvertently assists the poison's progress to the heart, Lillian and Navaz abetted my malignant increase as plainly as if they had taken me aside and said, 'Here, here is the weakest spot in the whole structure,' and, 'This is what I can never forgive, can never be compensated for.' This is the house which I continue to inhabit, even from a distance; its loss a pang, like aluminium on a dental filling. I made myself indispensable to its day-to-day functioning and was invited in by Lillian and Navaz, who gifted me upon themselves with all the slow pleasure of someone who thinks they have got something for nothing. My departure cracked that house open along its spine. I thought I was leaving as a thief might leave, with the most valuable object secure in my possession. As it turned out, I was being escorted from the premises to an exile in these four rooms, on whose bare walls I rerun short takes of scenes from miles away, from months ago. The lights go down and there is Lillian in her Jean Batten costume, scarf wired out from her neck as if caught in a slipstream.

Lillian liked to give parties. She would fill the house with people and move among them in her leather aviator's cap, goggles pushed high on her forehead, only talking to Navaz and me. Or she might invite to dinner a dozen friends who were strangers to each other, range them on either side of the kitchen table, and drive them through conversations like sheep over hurdles. The three of us did not sit together on these occasions which were, nevertheless, entirely staged for our pleasure. The afternoon of such a dinner party would find us all in the kitchen. Lillian, her face flushed with the stove's heat or excitement, is boning a rabbit, Navaz and I shelling peas. We decide in advance the topics for tonight's conversations. Navaz wants cross-dressing, then feminism in the public service but Lillian vetos this as too easy. We settle on cross-dressing followed by the sharemarket.

Lillian excels at these games. At the head of the table, her eyes shine in the candlelight. It is always she who makes the difficult transition, encouraging a certain line of talk when she sees long in advance that it might provide that crucial switchpoint. It is always she who pulls the new topic wriggling from the old while Navaz and I smile with a sweet and stupid satisfaction at our plates. At her best, she bullies one of her guests into making the crossover for her. One night, in imagined opposition to Lillian, one of the poets says, 'Cross-dressing has nothing to do with deviance. It's all a matter of give and take, supply and demand. You may as well say the sharemarket is an institution of perversity.'

I hang my smiling face over the roundness of my plate and know, without looking, that two seats down, on my right, Navaz is doing the same.

I can see now that these games were only childish. They were the games of the schoolyard, of best friends and girl gangs, of fierce quarter-hour loyalties. It is not clear to me why I was chosen to supplement that household. I was as unlike Lillian and Navaz as these others who were, at once, invited and scorned. Still, I was not above signalling to the other guests my special place in the house. As if casually, I would stand from the table and stir a saucepan on the stove or even leave the kitchen for a few minutes to watch the late news in the living room. And when it came time for that collective departure at the end of the night, I was always on this side of the front door, handing back coats, sometimes even being thanked, along with Lillian and Navaz, by voices that would call back up the drive in the dark. Then, for half an hour, I would sit with Lillian and Navaz at the cleared table, reviewing the evening's events, delaying the return to my aunt's house and the moment when that amused scrutiny might turn on me.

Even then, I knew the quick reversability of these alliances, that Lillian and Navaz's inexplicable affection for me was also a hostile indifference worn inside out. Now, cast up on this desk in a country that has never stopped being frightening for me, my aunt's photograph before me, I feel most painfully my exclusion from all that which once drew me in. I am Navaz's best translation. The same thing I always was, in this new register I am almost wholly unrecognisable. I am too tired for this. Although it is not yet midday, I go and lie down on my bed, fingers laced across my chest and stare past the slow-turning blades of the fan at the white square of the ceiling.

II

My memory is a twisted beast. It gives me back objects and postures I would hardly have thought I noticed the first time. It is in pieces, unable to tell me the story of my life, content to replay endless fragments, rounded off and separated from each other like beads on a string.

Just before Christmas, Lillian sends out invitations to a tattoo party. So everyone will know she is serious, she invites a painter who is well known for the Frida Kahlo *The Suicide of Dorothy Hale* he has tattooed in the rectangle between his nipples. Work on our own tattoos starts immediately. Lillian chooses for herself a red heart encircled with a scroll which carries the word *Mother*. She spends half a day at her work bench, drawing it onto a sheet of transparency, experimenting with different letterings. I remember the bald tattooist I assisted in Tonks Lane whose crowded skin was like Persian carpet and wonder if I can invite him without too much being made of our acquaintance. I am favouring the Emperor penguin from his right calf for my shoulder blade but, in the end, it is Navaz who chooses my tattoo, a da Vinci line drawing of Christ crucified. Soon this is pinned up next to Lillian's heart but the question of Navaz's tattoo has yet to be decided.

Lillian is working on something for days, her door closed against the rest of the house. When she finally shows us the third tattoo, it seems too large for Navaz's body. It is drawn on a piece of transparency nearly two and a half feet wide and is a detailed representation of an English fox hunt. It is not at all what I expected. In the background is the indistinct whiteness of the manor house, an extracted wisdom tooth on green baize. There is the green of the lawns, then the fields, crisscrossed by box hedges, and the woods. The closer to the lower edge of the transparency the more detail there is. The lawn around the house is a solid block of colour, the horsemen at the rear, red smears on their mounts. Mid-field, there is saliva glistening at the hounds' chops, the master of the hunt has a whisky nose. At the very forefront of the picture, two fields ahead of the leading horse and the pack of hounds boiling under its hooves, is the bright puff of the fox's tail, every orange hair distinctly drawn. Lillian's tattoo, even my tattoo, look like cartoons next to this scene.

This is also how, five flights up from the rest of the world, my memory works over my past. One scene is sketchily recalled as a line drawing; another is a cartoon, its simple shapes standing in for more complicated configurations; a third, seemingly no more significant than the others, I carry like a rolled up canvas, its detailed brushstrokes giving me back more than I knew was to be had.

On the afternoon that is a joke between us now, when Professor Mody asked fearfully, 'You are not Miss Betty, then?', I saw for the first time the British edition of Navaz's translation of *Skin Behind Bone*. When I confess to not being Miss Betty, there is a long silence that alarms even me. There seems little point in trying to reassure Professor Mody with my own name, which comes back to me quite formally on that low chair as 'Miss Helena'. I consider starting my explanation with my aunt and her postcards, that shot of her on the street corner with the professor hovering overhead on his balcony like an angel. Instead, moving slowly as if to soothe a nervous animal, I turn over the airmail envelope on the table in front of me and begin an even more complicated explanation that at no point accounts for my presence in this room.

The professor still has his hand to his throat. I watch his whitened knuckles and my voice goes out like a slow-motion lasso.

'This is a letter from Shio Nishimura,' I begin cautiously. 'He is the author of—' But Professor Mody's fingers have tightened again about his throat and he interrupts me, 'Yes, yes, Nishimura I have read. *The Glass Jaw. Skin Behind Bone. The Last Astronaut.*' The professor knows more of Nishimura than I do. He stares at the envelope on his table as if it might talk.

'Nishimura is writing to Navaz Nicholson,' I continue, wondering what explanation there might be for how I come by this correspondence. 'She is his translator.' The professor and I say these last two words together. Professor Mody is having trouble getting any words past his hand which still has him by the throat. He releases himself suddenly.

'Wait here. Wait here.' He throws himself from the room.

In a few minutes he is back with a copy of *Skin Behind Bone* that is unfamiliar to me.

'The best novelist writing today,' says the professor awkwardly, as if for promotional purposes. He places the book face down on the table beside my envelope. There are two photographs on the back cover. Professor Mody jabs his finger at the first one. It is a head and shoulders shot of a Japanese man, his generous face broad as a boat's oar.

'Nishimura,' announces the professor, before stabbing the picture opposite. 'Nicholson.' And it *is* Navaz, over Lillian's photo credit, her smile so small it is all in her eyes. She has one hand supporting the side of her head, fingers at her temple. In a pale shirt, its three top buttons undone, she is sitting outside somewhere, perhaps in the front garden at Raroa Road. The background is an out of focus blur of green. The professor and I smile fiercely at each other although ours cannot be the same happiness.

Even now when I think of Navaz's body what comes back to me most strongly, most intimately, is also that which is most public, that which any acquaintance or even stranger is free to gaze at. What moves me most about Navaz's remembered body are the prominent flare of her collarbones, the perfect dents of her temples. Everybody's collarbones are not beautiful; everybody does not have temples, just a general area of their heads where they might properly belong. Navaz's collarbones ride easily in the open V of her shirt. Her temples invite kisses: above her cheekbones and below her hairline, a steady pulse marks the spot.

On the morning of Lillian's tattoo party, the three of us are up early. With Lillian instructing her, Navaz traces the heart on to Lillian's bicep and carefully inks in its outlines. Lillian transfers the da Vinci to my shoulder blade and, sitting me in front of a mirror and holding up another behind like a barber, shows me her handiwork. Then the two of us begin work on Navaz. Wrapping the large transparency around Navaz's middle, Lillian shows me how the hunt will go. The manor house is above Navaz's left breast, the tardy hunters string across her belly and hip while all the action—the dogs, the horses and huntsmen—takes place at the small of her back.

Lillian takes a slow turn about Navaz, saying with some satisfaction, 'All that there is no better than what a fool Indian would do. It's a heap of vanity.' I assume a casualness that is not my own and busy myself with the inks and spirit-soaked sponges.

'Vanity of vanities,' says Lillian. Navaz takes off her shirt as if before surgeons.

I must have seen Navaz half-naked. I spent three hours bending over her body on Lillian's work bench, sponging away runnels of colour. Yet in all the time it took to make over Navaz's front as English countryside, to set the paint with Lillian's blowdryer, to roll her over and colour down her back, finishing with the fox's tail disappearing into the cleft of her buttocks, I can remember none of the detail that had me thick-tongued and clumsy that day, squeezing those green and red sponges until my own hands resembled some expressionistic rural carnage.

12

Our plane touches down at Santa Cruz airport in the dark. In the transit lounge at Singapore, Navaz goes into the toilet with her overnight bag. I do not recognise her when she comes out. The lounge is crowded with Indians and their duty-free shopping. They take up the front seats by the departure door so they can be first on to the plane, stowing their excess hand luggage under other people's seats. Navaz stands a moment in the toilet doorway and then walks towards me. I do not recognise her yet. This woman is wearing a long white cotton shift, overstitched in white, a pair of loose white trousers underneath with tight-fitting ankle cuffs. She wears leather sandals and her shirt is fastened at every button up to her chin. She is carrying Navaz's overnight bag. Navaz manages the short distance between us with careful steps, as if in high-heeled shoes. Even her walk is not her own.

I recognise this costume from a photograph Navaz has shown me of her relatives. Her cousin wears something very like it, but in a floral pattern with a contrasting waistcoat and scarf. There is something religious, almost surgical, about all this white. Navaz says nothing about her transformation. She stows her bag, which presumably now contains her jeans and shirt, under her seat and stares ahead of her as if at a constantly changing scene. I look surreptitiously at her neck where it emerges from her collar, at her hands lying in her lap. Her skin seems suddenly dark against the white cloth. In the transit lounge, I am alone.

During the flight, Navaz sleeps. The weight of her head on my shoulder is a comfort to me. Somewhere over the ocean, surrounded by strangers, she wakes and, the bones of her face still relaxed in sleep, asks some mumbled question. I hear 'What if they don't like me?' which rearranges itself inside my ear as 'What if they aren't like me?' A sweet anxiety creases her forehead but only for a moment, then she is awake, brushing her hair back from her face, slipping her sandals back on, checking for her passport. I squeeze her hand in mine but the moment for reassurance has passed. Navaz looks at me sharply as if I am the one enduring some half-concealed worry. The plane is descending in the darkness and sooner than I would have thought possible the lights of a city are visible beneath us.

'Look,' says Navaz, her small smile the only familiar thing about her. 'The real India.'

Although we would never admit to each other our belief in the real India, Prakash was to be our guide to that country. At nine-thirty, we are outside the Hotel Printravel, clean and ready for whatever he might show us. He arrives on time and has changed his clothes. Now he wears a white shirt like a bank teller and his proprietorial arranging of us in the back seat, his smoothing of his eyebrows with a wet finger in the wing mirror, persuades us that, whoever it was that drove us from the airport, this Prakash is assured, learned, almost urban. He does not leap up into the rickshaw as he did this morning but takes his seat, resting his hands, those polished hands, beside him on the vinyl for a few seconds, allowing a moment to insert itself between the ordinary business of the day and the tour.

The first stop is a water mill, just outside the town limits. Prakash hands us down from the rickshaw, taking particular care with our limbs, as if we are stick insects whose legs might be lost to careless handling. Navaz slips out gracefully. I feel clumsy under Prakash's touch and bark my shin on the side of the door, clip my head againt the overhang of the roof. Other drivers are now pulling up; other tourists, cameras swinging from their necks, are climbing down unassisted. Prakash ignores the other drivers, standing together in their shirt sleeves in the sun, and their much more ordinary cargoes. He steers us through the arched entrance.

The courtyard of the mill is cool and leafy, and full of the splashing of the water wheel that turns in the pool. We walk around its circumference while Prakash explains the workings of the grinding stones.

'A holy man is buried here,' says Prakash. 'A saint.' He leads us over to a white plastered hut which I had taken for a pump house.

'This is his tomb.' Prakash stands in front of the tomb, tucking his chin into his neck, once, twice, three times, like a duck. Navaz and I stand stiffly behind him.

'Do you have any money?' asks Prakash now. 'Any small coins?' Navaz pulls some coins from her pocket and hands them over.

'Come,' says Prakash and we walk around to the side of the tomb, to a blank wall, harshly white in the sun. Prakash presses one of the coins to the wall and when he removes his hand it stays there, glittering like a small mirror.

'There is no explanation for this,' says Prakash. 'Now you must try.' My coin does not stick. It falls from the wall as soon as I remove my hand.

'You are pressing too hard,' Prakash says. 'No pressure is needed. Just hold it to the wall, then take your hand away.' This time the coin stays there, shining next to Prakash's. Navaz is still trying. Prakash has his hand on hers, helping. He is shorter than her and he stands between her and the wall, her chin almost resting on his gleaming head. The coin stays. There are three of them, a shiny triangle on the white wall, and the three of us stand below, smiling at each other in the sun, as if we have succeeded in some trick or other.

'A holy place,' says Prakash, taking the coins down and handing them back to Navaz. 'And look.' He tilts his head back, we do the same and stare up into the blue square of sky that hangs over the walls of the mill like a roof. I can see nothing, only a blue of incalculable height.

'No bird ever flies over this enclosure,' says Prakash. 'They fly around. This is how we know it is a holy place.'

Prakash takes us to the doorway of the inner pool.

'Give me your camera, please. I will take your photo now,' he says in a businesslike way. Navaz and I stand woodenly, one on either side of the doorway, like topiary, as if we have never had our pictures taken before.

'Smiling or not smiling?' calls Prakash. Then he hands the camera to Navaz, arranging himself beside me for the next shot. He has produced from somewhere a pair of sunglasses with reflecting lenses and he puts these on. I have not moved from my side of the doorway but Prakash stands beside me. I feel his warmth at my hip. Then Navaz and I are obediently swapping places. Through the cross-hatched inner circle of the camera lens, I see Prakash take Navaz's hand in his own. His head comes up to her shoulder, he stands beside her like a schoolboy.

'Ready,' he calls through his teeth. This is to be a smiling photograph. I look again to where his hand holds hers, two brown hands gripping each other below shirt cuffs. I press the shutter and everything goes black.

On our way out, I see another group of three, a driver and a German couple in matching tracksuits, heads tilted back, looking up at the square blue sky. The wife is holding the husband's elbow as if the flat courtyard is a thin high ledge that she might pitch off at any moment. I hear the driver say 'No bird ever flies over this enclosure,' and the Germans take photographs of that pure blue, their cameras pointing straight up like the beaks of baby birds. Back at the rickshaw, I climb in the far side while Prakash assists Navaz in taking her seat. We are on our way to a famous hill fort, Prakash explains over his shoulder. There are green fields on either side of the road: for all I know we could be heading straight back to the airport. Navaz's hand lies between us on the seat, like something wounded. As the rickshaw begins to climb, I look back across the plain to where the dark smear of trees and white walls of the mill are still visible. I think I see a crow fly over the enclosure but, from this distance, it is hard to be sure.

The fort does not look like much from the road. It does not even look like a building but a huge side of red rock with a few dark holes that might be doors or windows. Prakash parks next to two buses that have passed us on our way here. Navaz and I leap down from the rickshaw before he can come around to help either of us but he is still sitting in the driver's seat, his sunglasses on top of his head like an extra set of eyes.

'This fort is built out of a rock,' Prakash explains, without looking at where it stands on the hillside. It seems he will not be coming inside with us. 'Give three rupees only for the guided visit,' he says. 'The man is a thief and will ask for more.'

It is like being let out of school early. We take the path that leads up to the fort, holding hands once we are round the first bend. A sleepy man stands behind a trestle table near the fort under a hand-lettered sign, *Govt Ap-proved Office*. He is wearing a khaki uniform like that of the Bombay policemen.

'Five rupees for exterior view,' he says, when he sees us coming. 'Seven rupees for guided tour inside and out.' We give the thief twenty rupees and let him keep the change. He is suddenly alert and runs after us as we make our way to where we can see the busloads of Americans assembling in front of the red rock. The ticketman, hardly recognisable now in his excitement, pushes us through to the front and introduces us to the guide.

'Our very special guests,' he says to this man. 'All the way from America.' Our fellow Americans take us in suspiciously. The guide says nothing, only clicks his torch on and off, before leading us all inside. The ticketman waves and waves, as if this dusty stretch of grass is a railway platform and he is seeing us now for the last time.

Inside, everything is dark. The Americans sound like cattle, lowing and shuffling their hooves in the darkness. The torch clicks on and our guide appears above us, his face illuminated from below by the beam of light. Two shadows blot out his eyes, his moustache clings to his upper lip like a bat. The Americans moan and squeak like a stand of trees. In the gloom, I make out Navaz's face on my right and shuffle over to her side.

'In the fourteenth century, when this fort was built,' announces the guide, 'the doorway that you just stepped through was a moat filled with cobras and crocodiles. Please step this way and we will see the rest of the fortifications.' We walk forward in the torch's ungenerous light, the front row stumbling on the steps cut into the rock.

'These passages which tunnel through the fort turn back on themselves at every bend so that invading soldiers would attack each other in the dark,' says the guide, holding his torch steady for the last of us to reach the stairs. And indeed, up ahead, some of the Americans have become disoriented and are trying to battle their way down the stairs against the flow of those continuing upwards. Our progress is further slowed by a low doorway which forces us to pass, one by one, on hands and knees. The guide, already on the other side of this door, explains that the defenders of the fort would stand where he stands, beheading the enemy as they obligingly stuck their heads through the gap. He chops playfully at one of the American necks in illustration.

Now the steps have run out, although the smooth-sided tunnel continues to climb. The guide is hurrying now. We are all scrambling behind him, no one wants to be left behind in the dark. He is telling us that boiling oil and red hot coals could be poured and rolled down this section of the tunnel. He continues to talk easily as he runs but we are out of breath and panting. Our heavy breathing sounds like some bullish Minotaur is loose in the tunnel. Suddenly we have stopped, each person walking into the back of the one ahead. The guide is shining his torch on two closed doors in the wall.

'Choose one,' he says to a woman in stretch slacks puffing before him. She pushes open the one on the right. It opens straight onto a sheer drop to the ground a hundred feet below. We stand blinking in the daylight, backing away from the drop. The woman, the same one, it turns out, that was chopped in the neck earlier, begins to cry, still standing in the gap, her hair lifted now by a slight breeze. Her husband guides her away to the back of the group. The guide is pleased with our performance. He throws open the second door. It, too, opens into the air like the other.

'One hundred and twelve feet,' he says happily. 'One hundred and twelve feet.' His hand describes a gruesome trajectory towards the earth.

He leads us some short distance back down the tunnel to where there is a third door concealed in the rock. This leads out onto the roof and a view in all directions of the surrounding country.

'Now the fort is yours,' he says, clicking the useless torch on and off dejectedly. The traumatised American has gathered a small group of women about her. They are quivering and clucking with indignation. *Absolutely irresponsible,* I hear one of them say, *I will be making a formal complaint.* The guide hears also and watches them nervously, plucking at his shirt collar with his fingers. I stand near the edge and look down across the rectangular roofs of the buses parked on the road to the gate where the ticketman can just be made out. He is back at his table but he is still waving, both arms now over his head, back and forth, back and forth, as if we are a plane coming in to land.

Back at the rickshaw, Prakash is asleep. He is lying on his back, his head resting on the front tyre. He has taken his shirt off and is lying inside it. I get there first and stare at his face, puffy in sleep, until Navaz arrives. With his glasses still on top of his head, and now these extra white arms flung out on either side of his own, he looks like a bug that has been squashed on the road.

'What's happened?'

'He's sleeping.' Prakash wakes up when he hears our voices. He hurries behind the rickshaw and does not reappear until he is tucked in, buttoned up.

'You have seen the fort?' asks Prakash. We nod, climbing into the back seat. There is a patch of red dust on the back of Prakash's shirt, between his shoulderblades.

'The crocodile moat?' We nod again. Prakash starts the engine.

'And the loop tunnel? The trick doors?' We agree to everything.

'And you only paid three rupees each?' Prakash is looking over his shoulder. I haven't stopped nodding for the last question. I look across at Navaz whose head is moving up and down, up and down, like a sewing machine needle.

13

At Santa Cruz airport, we are last off the plane. There are no luggage trolleys left for us. The customs officials are already calling to one another as we walk away from the checkpoint, slow with the weight of our luggage. Over Navaz's shoulder, I can see her relatives. Standing in the gateway ahead, their toes to the red lettering on the linoleum, *Illegal to cross this point*, they are arranged exactly as they are in the photograph where the cousin is wearing the floral outfit, scarf and waistcoat. The two cousins flank their mother. They are a head taller than her and wearing Western clothes, a frock, a two-piece suit, as if they were a national costume. Navaz's aunt is wearing a sari. As in the photograph, she supports herself on the arms of her children like a gymnast on parallel bars. Navaz reaches them first and, as she turns to introduce me, I see at once the photograph that never was. It is as if I am being picked up at the airport by three cousins and the aunt.

My bags are lifted from me, a luggage trolley is found. We are moving out of the airport and into the carpark where the tops of cars are slowly colouring in the early light. Ahead of me, Navaz bends over her aunt in conversation. I see the aunt slip her hand into Navaz's. As I follow, a small, dry hand takes mine. I look down at an impossible face, a capsized mouth is working but no sound is coming out. I try to work my hand free but the grip is steady and not to be broken gently. The cousins are pushing the trolley towards a black taxi; Navaz and her aunt continue their talk. I lower my ear to that hollow mouth, wet as an octopus sucker, and hear its thin, breathy request, *chocolate, chocolate*. I have no chocolate, no Indian money even. I pat my empty pocket with my free hand but there is no interest in this pantomime. The mouth continues to chew over its silent *chocolate*. Navaz's aunt turns at the taxi, looks across the carpark for me. She walks across and, still talking to Navaz over her shoulder, disengages that grasping hand as I might knock a stone from my shoe. As our taxi moves from the stand, I see the real India taking up her place again at the double doors of the airport.

I have not been back to the international airport although, when Navaz left me, I made that return journey as surely as if it had been me who checked that the luggage was secure in the trunk; who handed out the last unwanted coins to the skateboard beggars at the traffic lights; who mentioned the name of the aunt's cousin when the man at check-in said, 'Excess baggage.' I remember these things as I remember everything else that has happened to me. I had not been able to kiss Navaz again in the hard light of the yard and, on the brink of departure, what good were such kisses that stopped the mouth? Still, Navaz's mouth seemed stopped with something. She stood next to me, looking down the lane to where the taxi would swing in from the road, as once she had looked out her study window, making herself blank for that perfect phrase. She stood beside me politely; there is no other word for it. Like strangers, we stood there. I caught up her suitcase, although it was too heavy to carry comfortably, and pressed it against my chest like a poultice.

Somehow, then, she was in the taxi—did I say the taxi had arrived?—and I was on the wrong side of the glass, seeing my face reflected in the pane and beyond that the dim smudge of Navaz. She had a smile such as I had never seen on her before, huge and gaping like an ulcer. It was the smile that took the place of words. The taxi drove out of the yard, sticking for a moment at the furthest reach of the lane, like a cork in a bottle. For the last time, I saw the shadow of her head through the rear window. Then I turned and climbed the stair. I can hardly say what it was like. A sentence presented itself to me on the second landing: *a body cannot sustain this*. Yet my heart kept up its even beating, the muscles in my legs contracted and relaxed on every step, I could count backwards from ten. As Navaz's taxi drove down the hill, swerved around a vegetable cart outside Kamal's, I let myself into the apartment, lowered myself onto the bed like a flag. I felt like the science teacher's experiment the second before the oxygen burned out in the belljar and the candle flame hesitated, went out.

Lost in our rooms, which were suddenly *mine*, I imagined Navaz's backwards journey. I saw her driving past the white burst of Haji Ali's tomb; I saw her, departure card in hand, step past *Illegal to pass this point.* When I woke, my windows were dark squares hanging over the night yard. My dreams had not quite left me, they lay across my skin like cobwebs. They seemed foreign somehow, not set in another country but like someone else's. My watch lay on the bedside table: three-thirty. I thought about time zones and flight paths. By my calculation, Navaz had left Singapore for Sydney, was slicing through the sky, trailing a white streak that fades like the scar on ice left by a skate's blade. I was like that celestial exhaust: left behind, tremulous, on the point of dispersion. In the morning, my watch still read three-thirty and I imagined Navaz's plane stalled against the sky, flung high and fastened there like a brooch.

14

In my fifth floor rooms overlooking the courtyard, I think back to the beginning of all this and come up against another beginning, the beginning of Nishimura's fourth novel. Then, Lillian, Navaz and I were all living in the same house, I want to say *happily*, though I have not forgotten the sometimes accusations, the tearful recriminations. I had yet to learn that a three is always a two and a one. (A three is always a two and a one.) In the remembered event, it is as it always is. Lillian is in the kitchen, Navaz is in her study and I am moving down the corridor between them like a beautiful translation. Navaz is looking out the window but, when she sees me in the doorway, she puts down her cigarette, takes up a sheet of blue airmail paper and reads me a line. *The man who is walking down the street is a man you know.* She does not sound like Navaz. Her voice is oddly measured and takes a slow pleasure in its modulation, like the voice of the man at home who, every year at my father's Christmas party, gives a recitation of Thomas Wyatt's 'Mine Own John Poins'. *The man who is walking down the street is a man you know.* I do not know what to make of this performance so I hang off the door jamb, happy enough to see the pencil tucked over Navaz's ear, to hear her new voice.

'I have been waiting for this.' Navaz has her usual voice again. 'It's Nishimura's latest novel.'

I make a joke. 'It's very short.' It doesn't seem like a very good opening line to me although Navaz is as pleased with it as if she wrote it herself. She is holding the paper up to the light as if some other truth is readable between the lines. It doesn't even sound as if it has quite been translated. It sounds like a sentence from a phrasebook. The man who is walking down the street illustrates some grammatical point. Navaz reads the line one more time, her voice rising and falling like a fishing buoy fixed to some unseen weight, like the voice of the man at the Christmas party when he says, *No man doth mark whereso I ride or go.*

Alone in my four rooms, I have started to talk to myself. I say the kind of things I might like to hear. *You're doing all right*, I said one morning when the sight of my teacup beside the typewriter forced a small and unexpected happiness from me. *There's plenty who are worse off.* I tried that once but it came out like something my mother would say. My voice sounds at once strange and familiar, mine and not mine, like a childhood photograph. I have started talking aloud to keep myself company. Sometimes my sentences are strangely emphasised which leaves me wondering what exactly it was that I meant. One afternoon I checked the mailbox Navaz had hired at the post office. Just as I was about to swing shut that little tin door, a thin blue envelope was inserted from the other side. *The best of* both *possible worlds*, I said, as if being disappointed by an empty postbox was one pleasure, receiving a letter simply another. I talk to Navaz even though I know she is no longer interested. I don't say the sort of thing you might expect, *you shouldn't have left me, why don't you write?* It's the ordinary things I miss. I call out from the kitchen, *do you want a cup of tea, I'm making one.* Once I even said, *cup of tea, love?* although I never called her that. *Love* was Navaz's word. It thrilled me that she could so easily say, *Bye love* when finishing a phone call, or ask in the dark, *Baby, are you awake?*

This morning I had breakfast at my desk holding *The Times of India* high and imagining Navaz sitting just across from me, a breath away, buttering her crusts and listening to me read from the paper. Before she left, I would often read aloud from the newspaper. Once I read a letter to the editor complaining about the bandicoot that had recently been observed running through the intensive care ward at Breach Candy Hospital. *Dear Sir, I take up my pen in protest.* Navaz would say this to me then, when I would interrupt her work or wake her, sliding my tongue along the creases at the back of her neck, *Dear Sir, I take up my pen in protest.* Then there were always the Rama Raos, a mysterious family who we never quite understood although every morning I would comb the paper looking for further news of their exploits. They first came to our attention in the coverage of a local election in some southern state we were later to pass through. The popular candidate Mr T. Rama Rao had been stabbed by Mr M.

Rama Rao in a dispute following a public debate. I was down to the last of the newspaper, reading even the crowded print on the last few pages, keeping Navaz at the table, her dressing-gown falling open at her neck, her cigarette pointed straight upwards as she listened, one thumb to her eyebrow. Two days later, it was announced that Mr T. Rama Rao was in a satisfactory condition, Mr M. Rama Rao's bail had been paid by Mr S. Rama Rao. *The Times of India* became the *Rama Rao Gazette* and every morning I read the paper from front page to back.

There had been no letter from Nishimura in eight days before I realised that the novel was finished. What I now recognised as Nishimura's last sentence was no more likely than his opening line. I had returned empty handed from Navaz's postbox five times before I knew the novel was finished. Looking into the tin postbox for the fifth time was like seeing the courtyard the moment after Navaz's taxi had pulled out into the street. I knew at once the vampiric emptiness that would start to feed on me, hollowing me out from within. Standing in the doorway of the post office, the buses changing down gears at the corner on their way to Breach Candy Hospital, I rattled in my fist the useless key, which I might as well have thrown away or swallowed. My voice, pitched for firmness, sounded weak against the traffic. I said to myself, 'It's over,' meaning nothing more than the novel but knowing at the same moment how that nameless novel named me. Nishimura's story of the Japanese medical student and the rooming house had been writing my days here. Without the certainty of those blue pages, what reason was there for my staying on; what reason for calling in at Professor Mody's apartment between seven and eight; for bending over my felted card table, knowing how, in the days to follow, Navaz would also bend over these same pages at that other table over the garden.

It was Lillian, not Navaz, who invited me to move in to their house. This is perhaps not as surprising as it seemed to me then. Navaz, after all, never said anything; it was always Lillian who arranged things, laid plans, who made the difficult transition. Late one night, after all the guests had left, the dishes still not done in the kitchen, we were watching television. Rather, we were drinking brandy from the dinner wine glasses, talking that lazy talk a television makes possible, not watching but allowing its soundtrack to take up any slack in our conversation. I was about to leave, had been about to leave for the last hour.

'Leave the dishes,' I said, although there was no danger of their being done. 'I'll come over in the morning and help you with them.'

'Stay,' said Lillian, with the same casualness that she usually said, *Goodnight*. She lead me not to the front door but back down the corridor to the spare room where the single bed was already made up and turned back, where the bedside lamp cast a pool of light across the pillows banked against the wall.

'Stay,' said Lillian again, as if training a dog. I slipped naked into that bed as easily as if I had slept there every night of my life. I left the lamp on for a while, listening to Lillian and Navaz moving about the house, water in the pipes, then silence. In the morning I felt unaccountably shy, too big for my skin, as I had the next time I saw Eunice, Mrs O'Malley, her names catching at the back of my throat. The following evening, I gathered my few things together when I came in from work. I locked my aunt's house for the last time, posted her keys through the slot for letters, and let myself in next door, feeling already quite at home.

The three of us never spoke about my shift: I did not express my gratitude to Lillian and Navaz for their invitation, they did not thank me for my acceptance. We knew we were getting away with something, to speak of it would be unlucky. It would be an exaggeration to say that things continued as usual. Now that I was living in the house, no longer simply a visitor, I occupied that space differently. I did the same things—talked to Lillian in the kitchen; hung off the door jamb, watching Navaz in her study; arranged the seating for the dinner parties—but with peculiar investment, like someone faking an accent. I began to see myself, I was going to say, as others saw me, but that's not quite right. I began to see myself through the lens of Lillian's camera. I became self-conscious, aware of myself, not in any awkward way, but in a series of smooth framings. I was always being set up, caught, in a doorway or through the window of Navaz's study, in the wash of light from my bedside lamp, between Lillian and Navaz at the table. My clothes fell on me in a new way. Light bloomed on my skin. I grew so sensitive that I could feel the changes in air pressure as Lillian or Navaz moved about in the other rooms. I did not need to ask myself if I was happy. I started to work in the garden outside Navaz's window. I slept without dreams in my single bed.

15

One afternoon, there is a knock at my apartment door. I am lying on my bed, covered only by a thin sheet, watching the blades of the fan turning overhead. For a moment I have forgotten what that noise is, a knock at the door. Navaz's family are still in Matheran; no one else knows where I am. I pull on some trousers, my shirt sleeves are caught inside out, my sandals are in the other room. Perhaps my aunt has come for me as she does in my imagination. Perhaps while I was counting the slow revolutions of the fan, she was walking up the lane towards the apartment, limping against the weight of her suitcase. Now she stands outside my front door as once I stood before hers, straddling her suitcase with an easy assurance. There is another knock. I am dressed now and standing in front of the door, uneasy about opening it, yet anxious that whoever it is might leave. I do not let myself think that it might be Navaz on the other side, separated from me by the width of a door. And not letting myself think of her, I see her at once as clearly as if there were no closed door between us. She appears as she does in the photograph at Professor Mody's apartment, a white shirt open against her skin, one hand raised to the side of her head, that negligible smile. I am suddenly small and ordinary, my sandals unbuckled, my cuffs flapping. Navaz will not care about any of that. She will cross the threshhold, right foot first for luck, touch me, make me valuable again. She will take me to bed, remove all her clothes as other people roll up their sleeves, seriously and with intent. She will push me against the mattress, unbutton, unbelt me and have me like that, in parts, her mouth and hands moving under my clothes. There is no time to push the beds together, no point in my closing the curtains, which are too thin to be any protection against the light. I am undone.

It is not Navaz, of course. It is not even my aunt. On the landing is a woman I have not seen before. At first I think she is one of the road menders I have seen outside Professor Mody's apartment, she wears the same clothes but is not so dusty. She seems surprised to see me and looks around the door jamb for someone else. I cannot understand what she is saying, she cannot understand me. Nevertheless, we continue to speak to each other for form's sake. I say, *Can I help you?* and *I am alone here.* I sound like my phrasebook. It makes no difference so I say, *You must go and get an undertaker. He lost all his property last night.* The woman says whatever it is that she is saying, covers her mouth with her hands and laughs. I want to ask her in but when I stand aside from the door so she can pass, she takes a step back. I want to make her a cup of tea, show her how I am living, point out my things for her—*typewriter, gas ring, bed*—even while I recognise such a desire as absurd. When she steps back from my doorway, I see that she has brought a large covered container up the stairs. It is plastic with handles, like a rubbish bin from home. At least I can buy something from her. I point at the bin, she nods, she also points, I raise the lid, it is empty. There is nothing to be done. She takes up her bin and climbs the stairs to the next floor. I close my door, lie on my bed again.

I can no longer interest myself in the turning of the fan. I wonder about the woman and her empty bin. I do not know what I expected to find in there although, just as I was unfastening the lid, I thought wildly, *snakes*. Perhaps some fish or religious postcards, metal *thali* trays, something we could have made some easy transaction over. Surely the bin itself was not for sale, since there was only one. She must have wanted to take something away from here, rubbish or clothes for the laundry. If Navaz were here, they could have spoken together while I stood aside, waiting for the door to be closed and the intimacy of the private translation. Still, while Navaz was still here, I could sometimes find these mediations estranging. We would have dinner with her family most nights. One or other of her cousins would come for us in the new Maruti or we would catch a taxi across town. The doors would be open to the balcony and we would sit to dinner late when the air was a little cooler. I would be made welcome, plied with food and complimented on my figure, but it was always a being *made* welcome. Soon the polite English of the schoolroom and the public service gave way to an easier, unknown language and for the rest of the evening I would be caught in a time lag, waiting for Navaz's hurried summaries of the conversation, laughing uneasily and alone after everyone had finished with the joke. Navaz's aunt would slip consolatory food on to my plate, the most tender cutlet, chutney from Kashmir, but I left each night exhausted as though I had watched six hours of subtitled films.

One night when we arrive, there are no places set for us. Navaz's aunt is plump with excitement.

'Tonight you are going out to dinner with some young people,' she says. 'I have arranged everything. You do not want always to be stuck with us. You are missing friends of your own age.'

Navaz's cousins say nothing, although they are both younger than Navaz and only a few years older than me. Navaz and I look at each other. The aunt is waiting for something.

'We enjoy eating with you,' I say which is not, for me, at least, exactly true, although they are suddenly a more managable prospect than the alarming thought of *young people*. The aunt seems pleased enough with such a response, although she brushes it aside with one contemptuous hand.

'No,' she says, her hand indicating her own family in a disparaging half circle, 'these young people are the jet set.' She says *jet set* in a peculiarly self-satisfied way, pronouncing it carefully as if it is a phrase in a more valuable language.

One of the jet set arrives to pick us up. His name is Rohan. He calls Navaz's aunt *Auntie* although he is no relation. He is a lawyer—'a barrister and a solicitor,' says Navaz's aunt—and, although technically a 'young person', he has the thinning hair and thickening body of a forty-year-old. He tells us that his car is downstairs, that he has been to America.

'I will bring them back safe-safe, Auntie,' he says at the front door. From behind the wrought-iron screen of the elevator, I see Navaz's aunt hug herself in pleasure. Rohan takes us to collect his girlfriend, Soona. He calls her his girlfriend but later that night Navaz's aunt refers to her as 'Rohan's fiancée.' Rohan leads Navaz and me up a flight of outside stairs to a door on the second floor.

He knocks at the door, above a sign which reads *Soona's Place. For Beauty with Style*. The door is opened by a slight woman in jeans and a tucked-in blouse. This is Soona, the 'modern girl', who carries her inverted commas carefully on either side of her bobbed head. Rohan takes her in his arms in the doorway and they kiss intently. Their jaws work up and down as if they are chewing. Navaz and I watch them. I wonder if the tongue can still go in and out when the teeth are opening and closing like that. It is all over quite quickly. Rohan and Soona smile at us with their eyebrows raised enquiringly. It is as if they have been auditioning for something.

'This is Soona,' says Rohan, one arm slung across her narrow shoulders, waving us inside. 'She is a beautician.' We are standing in Soona's salon, mirrored walls, black and white tiled floor. There are price charts up on the walls, *whole leg, half leg, bikini*. Soona invites Navaz to try out her reclining chair. Reflected before me, I see Navaz lying down, Soona bent over her face like a dentist. Rohan stands back, distancing himself from all this business but nevertheless taking up a proprietary stance at the door, hands in pockets and smiling like a lucky man. In the mirror, I am frowsy and unattractive. I am standing off to one side, alone and palely loitering. Soona locks the door and leads us through the house. In the living room, sitting silently on either side of a mosaic-topped coffee table are a man and a woman. I assume these are Soona's parents; they remind me troublingly of my own. Soona's father, if that is who he is, raises one slow palm like a pointsman on duty. I stop obediently but it turns out to be a silent greeting.

'Hello,' I say foolishly, but there are to be no introductions. The others are waiting for me at the open front door.

We are going to a restaurant for dinner but first we stop at another apartment building.

'The gang are all meeting here,' explains Rohan, *the gang* sounding believable, even enviable, in his mouth. More flights of stairs, another front door, although this time there are marbled landings and potted palms. Rohan rings the doorbell and there is a frenzied scrabbling and barking from inside and a woman's voice calling, 'No, Bumbum! O, Bumbum!' The door opens and there is a woman with made-up face and long loose hair, looking more like a beautician than Soona does, throwing herself first on Rohan and then on Soona but pulling up short at the sight of Navaz and me behind them, still calling, 'O see what Bumbum's done.' There is a small puddle of urine in the hall which no one seems really to mind. Bumbum is a kind of mad half-dog, churning about our feet like a wind-up bath toy. He is, I suppose, a dachshund but his back legs are paralysed. He pulls himself along the marble floor with his front legs, his back half fishtailing uselessly from side to side. Aafreed introduces herself, or rather, she puts a hand to her chest and says, 'Aafreed,' as if she were an obvious conclusion waiting to be drawn. She does not bother with our names, or perhaps she already knows them. She walks us through the house, past another set of parents sitting ignored and uncomplaining in the living room, Bumbum wheeling and skidding at our side.

Aafreed takes us to her bedroom which is already crowded like a doctor's waiting room. Everything is pink and frilled, even the lampshade, but the jet set is squashed in here with an almost nightclub-like sophistication. There are another four men and three women, who I manage to sort into couples during the evening, although I never match them with their names. Aafreed makes another disaffected introduction. It seems that apart from Soona and Rohan, all the others are air stewards in the same international airline. They are sitting along the two single beds, among the stuffed toys, drinking Jim Beam from shot glasses.

'Duty free,' says a man, who I think is called TJ, raising his glass as if in a toast. TJ, if that is his name, is master of this kind of cul de sac comment. Later, at the restaurant, he wags his chicken bone across the table at one or other of the stewards, and says to me, 'Charles, now he is a Christian.' When I seem unimpressed by such accomplishment, TJ puts his face even closer to mine and adds, 'Born, not converted.' But for now, Navaz and I are wedged onto opposite beds, glasses of Jim Beam in hand. Aafreed and another woman whirl in and out of an adjoining bathroom, sometimes letting Bumbum in with them, sometimes shutting him out, changing their clothes while the gang decide what looks best.

Unnoticed by anyone else, Navaz is smiling her tiny smile and, as I did at Raroa Road, I feel chosen, picked out, special. At last, we leave for the restaurant. We walk past the arched entrance to the living room, Bumbum giving short yelps, his nails clattering over the marble, but the parents do not turn their heads. At the door, Aafreed looks at Bumbum and says to me, as if in response to some question, 'Car accident.'

The restaurant is just around the corner from our apartment. I pass it every time I walk to the post office. Now it is called *Fine Times* but then it was more obscurely *My Delicious* or *My Delirious*, I can't remember. Its plate glass windows faced on to the street and inside the known and would-be-known shone. Our party was shown to the largest table in the centre of the room and we walked in like film stars, the men's shirts unbuttoned at the collar, some of the women in trousers. The chef himself comes out to see us, slapping the waiter away with a white cloth he had tucked up in his apron strings. He knows Aafreed and asks after her parents.

'And Bumbum?' he asks, his voice low with concern. The chef has taken the waiter's order book from him and now he waits, pencil raised, to take our orders while the waiter scowls from behind the porthole window of the kitchen swing door.

'Tonight we have the finance minister,' the chef says, nodding discreetly across the room, as if this were the speciality of the day. 'The young lady is not his wife.'

Once the order has been taken, the gang work to regain control of the room. They snap their fingers at the waiter and order imported beers, insisting that Navaz and I drink a local cashew liquor which has to be sent out for. The airline stewards talk loudly about their flight rosters: they say Paris, London, Copenhagen, New York, Chicago.

'What are Americans like?' asks Rohan, forgetting that he has already told us that he has been there. The steward who is currently on the American circuit looks thoughtful for a moment.

'They're like her,' he says, pointing down to the end of the table where I am sitting.

'Dear Sir,' I say, leaning across to Navaz, 'I take up my pen in protest.' Navaz does not smile. She does not seem to hear. She is looking at me carefully, head on one side, calculating my Americanness.

16

Professor Mody never asks how I come by Nishimura's letters to Navaz. After that first day when he established that the correspondence was genuine, he has had nothing more to say on the subject. When I call on him, I bring the latest sheet of airmail paper. Professor Mody removes this paper from its envelope using the very tips of his fingers. He flattens the paper against the surface of the coffee table and hangs over it intently, as if over a baby in a crib. At these moments, he smiles a shy smile; he rocks back from the page and repeats certain phrases to me, phrases which I sometimes, and perversely, delete that very night before forwarding the work to Navaz. The professor is a little in love with Nishimura. We are a fine couple.

'"The entrails' sure clutch,"' says the professor. '"Innocent as an egg."' He strokes these phrases with a careful forefinger. His eyes shine as if glazed.

'Excuse me,' says Professor Mody, not routinely, as if leaving a table, but as one who has said too much. Nevertheless, he does leave the table, goes out to the kitchen to prepare our supper. It is left to me to put away Nishimura's letter.

The professor returns with the beer and the salted cashews I had brought. He puts the nuts, still in their smeary twist of newspaper, on the far side of the table. He returns to the kitchen while I pour two slow glasses, the warmth of my hand making the frosted bottle drip. Professor Mody returns with some orange confectionary piled on a silver plate.

'I had these made particularly.' I think he means 'specially', but, since we are still careful with each other, I say nothing. I would prefer the taste of salt with the beer but the nuts are still wrapped, not in their usual bowl.

'You would prefer the nuts?' Professor Mody holds the sweets under my nose and I select the smallest one. It is bigger than it looks, an orange coil, sticky under my fingers, and warm, which I hadn't expected. It is very sweet and oozes an oily syrup. The beer tastes slightly metallic after so much sugar but it is not unpleasant letting the sweet oil spread across the back of my tongue, drinking with the professor. Only Professor Mody is not drinking. He has not yet sat down. He is running a careful finger across the spines of the books in his bookshelf, selecting a slim, cloth-bound volume. He is saying, 'Miss Betty and I are translating some of Yukio's erotic verse at the moment. Do you know it?'

I have the grace to look thoughtful, as if considering the range of Japanese erotica familiar to me. There is no need for any answer for across the room the professor is readying himself for his reading. He has the book open and held at an awkward half-arm's length from his face. His feet are in the ballet dancer's first position. He looks like an illustration for *declamation* in a children's encyclopaedia. The fountain falls; the professor waits. To defend myself against the weight of expectation, I continue to convey the bright sweets from plate to mouth, raise my glass frequently for short sips, knock it reassuringly against the table as I put it back down. Professor Mody begins to read. At first, I do not listen to him. He holds himself at an angle that allows me to watch him unguardedly and he speaks in that slow, steadily groping voice that I have come to associate with translation. He is wearing his usual safari suit, he holds himself upright, but—is it just my imagination—does he seem looser, somehow unbuttoned?

'Take these kisses from my nether lips,' reads the professor, the hesitation before *nether* seeming to be connected to terminology rather than propriety. Professor Mody is not unattractive at this angle and after a little beer. He has a carefulness about him that I find reassuring; there is a handkerchief folded in his breast pocket, his nails are clean and neatly squared off. When he cannot immediately come up with the right word, he holds his mouth open and cocks his head to one side as if he might dislodge it from somewhere higher up in his head. He reads everything in the same even voice. 'My wet thighs,' says the professor without a trace of irony. I wonder if this is how he would imagine a seduction. Certainly he would not force himself on me while I sat at his low table, would not push me up against the wall when I stood to leave.

'If it had tongue,' says the professor, 'My slot of joy/ barely would know whether to urge/ you to action or voiceless wait/ a silent invitation to your splendid machine.'

Those are the last lines. Professor Mody waits a fraction longer, listening in silence to his voice continuing like a tuning fork. He fusses for a moment at the shelf, replacing the book, easing it into line with the others. Then he takes his seat across the table, his eyes fix on mine over the rim of his glass. Clearly, something is expected of me.

'*Tongueless*,' I say. '*Or tongueless wait* would have been better.' Professor Mody's eyes are dark and moist as his beer.

'I already used *tongue*,' he says reproachfully.

Navaz first kissed me some time in November. I remember the tomato plants were big enough for me to have started pinching out their lateral shoots. It was almost dark. The last light of the day was concentrated in the heads of the marigolds which flared orange and yellow in the shadowy troughs between the tomatoes. The light in Navaz's study was already on and, pretending not to look, I could see her in the window, staring across to the street, a dark head in a yellow square. I was a single ghost at the bottom of the garden, my thin T-shirt streaked with earth, the green fur of the tomato stalks under my fingernails. The house was lit up like a pumpkin. Then Navaz was no longer at her window, which continued to gleam emptily like an eye put out. She was framed a moment in the open front door, she was coming down the front steps and I saw for the first time how someone might *descend a staircase*. She stood beside me and together we looked at the dark square of the garden. My fingers smelled of tomatoes. Navaz took my head in her hands as if it were the first fruit of the season, pressed her lips against my forehead and then, less carefully, against my mouth. She walked up the front steps and, standing where she left me, I heard the water being drawn for my evening bath. I felt about in the dark for the rake and hoe, thrilling myself over and over with the thought of Navaz's smoky mouth, her hands over my ears, the sounds of the garden lost to the rush of my own blood. Inside the house everything was the same. Floating in the bath, I knew what I pretended not to know: the kiss on my forehead was a blessing, the kiss on my lips a dangerous promise.

Professor Mody asks me to visit him around noon the following day. There is no new page from Nishimura; I carry my bundle of spiced nuts before me like an alibi. The professor does not even bother to take them from me. He has a light jacket on over his safari suit.

'We are going out,' he says. He does not dare look at me but tucks his head down and smooths the front of his suit. I also do not look at him. I pretend that this is more or less what I had expected. I follow him down the stairs and wait outside on the pavement while he locks the door. In the taxi, I ask, 'Where are you taking me?' but this has an unwanted note of tremulousness so I say instead, 'Where are we going?' The professor does not notice the difference, or prefers the idea of an abduction, for he says, 'I am taking you to a house, a good house, where we will have our backs done.' We drive on in silence, well past the range of my familiar territory, the driver hunched over the wheel like the mad manservant in a horror movie.

17

The house is just that, a house. It is in an area of the city I have not been to before. While Professor Mody hands money to the taxi driver and waves away the change with an impatient hand, I look at the white stone front, the dark front door. It is not as bad as I had imagined in the taxi, although my worst scenario is tame enough, straight from one of the Hindi movies Navaz and I once watched with her cousins where the vamp always had her hands on her hips and blew cigarette smoke out her nose. The professor guides me up the few steps to the front door, one hand not quite on the small of my back. A pale shape is moving towards us up the corridor and I realise that the door is not shut at all but opens wide onto the house's dark interior. In the taxi, as my familiar city slipped away, I made a series of resolutions: *I will not be separated from Professor Mody; I will only watch the professor have his back done; I will not remove my shirt and underpants; I will not be left alone with the professor.* Now, standing between the professor and this white-smocked woman, my back warmed by the heat rising from the street, my face cool in the light breath the house exhales, such resolutions feel less unnecessary than impossible.

The woman in white—there is something so understatedly clinical about the house, I almost want to say 'the nurse'—sits me in front of a desk in the reception area and takes some details. This is how she describes it.

'If I might just take some details?' she says with delicacy, as if it were money or blood that she were taking. Professor Mody, whose details presumably have already been taken, removes himself a discreet distance, stands at the window overlooking the street with his hands clasped behind his back.

'Date of birth?' asks the woman, her voice going up at the end like a fishhook, her pen and eyebrows raised as she waits for my reply. My name is printed in block capitals across the top of the filing card.

'Weight? Height? How long have you known the professor?' She jerks her head slyly in Professor Mody's direction at the last question and does not make a note of my answer.

Once I am documented and filed in alphabetical order, the woman leads the professor and me upstairs to a large room, well-lit, with two examination couches side by side in the centre. She hands us both loose cotton gowns, such as are worn before an operation, and directs us to a pair of cubicles against the far wall.

'Slip off your clothes, please,' she says, making it sound as if our clothes have been an unwelcome imposition from the start, as if it would only take a slight relaxing of the will to have them falling from us like leaves. My resolutions are in tatters but, in the privacy of my cubicle, I assert myself by scrupulously folding all my clothes. When I emerge, Professor Mody is laid out on his belly, in his gown, and the masseuse, for it turns out that this is what she is, is standing between the couches waiting for me. I lie on my couch just as the professor is lying on his, belly down, chin on my crossed arms. The masseuse moves to the top of my couch, holds my head in her hands for a moment as if about to baptise me. Then the buttons of my gown, which I have taken care to fasten, from the backs of my knees to my neck, are undone one by one.

With my gown hanging down on both sides of the couch like broken wings, I hear rather than see Professor Mody turn his head to look at me. The masseuse runs her fingers through my hair, wrinkling and smoothing my scalp under her hands. She rubs her palm along the base of my skull, picks up the folds of skin at the back of my neck and rolls them, like a cloth merchant, between thumb and forefinger. The whole length of my body cleaves to the couch in anticipation of her meticulous descent. I make myself imagine the maid making the medical student's back. Would it be like this, skin on skin? Would the maid's fingers have the strength of these that pummel my shoulderblades, knocking the breath from me in short puffs, or would she be gentler, tracking her small breasts in the groove of Sanki's back? But the maid does not get to touch Sanki at all. She is sent away to complete her chores. It is the frightening bulk of Mr Oliver who shoves himself up from the head of the table and—dragging the medical student, still seated in his chair, away from the table—claims that back for himself.

When I think of Mr Oliver I have an image of loutish strength which I am not sure he deserves. In the maid's description, which is all I have to go on, he is tall certainly and broad across the chest, *the kitchen cracks and heaves like a whip when Mr Oliver walks from door to sink.* Still, I think there may be another side to Mr Oliver. I imagine the fierce tenderness that confounds him when he finds himself between Sanki and the maid, when he stands in the yellow light of the back door watching Sanki bent over the dark square of freshly turned earth, the maid moving about behind him in the kitchen, singing as she puts away the dishes. After all, I know what it is to want something you ought not want; I know what it is to try and save yourself by making that thing diminish until, so small it is almost invisible, it inflicts itself on you at every moment like dust under your eyelid. Perhaps, after all, it is Mr Oliver who would massage Sanki like this, his hands counting down the ribs to the last smooth curve before the buttocks' swell. His hands would be not only strong, like these on my back, but large, encompassing the medical student's narrow hips in a single span.

I stare over my fists at the line the wall makes where it meets the floor. The masseuse is kneading the small of my back; every now and then I feel her sleeve drag across my bare skin. I think again of Nishimura's unlikely last line: *The table is wiped, the chairs put up for the night; she will choose the one who is least like her.* The hands move to my buttocks and that intake of breath is Professor Mody's. No wonder I waited for the next page and, when it was late, waited for it still. For the first three days, when there was no thought in my mind but that another pale blue page would arrive, I barely considered the matter. *She will choose the one who is least like her.* In idle moments, I decided first one way and then another. The maid would, of course, choose Sanki because she and Mr Oliver are both Scottish and permanent residents of the boarding house. She would naturally choose Mr Oliver since Sanki is young and, like her, has a sense of himself to grow into. Mr Oliver and the maid both enjoy the medical student. They move each other through their shifting claims on him. Sanki and the maid are both sidelined in any official description of the household. Foreigner and hired help, they watch each other through the kitchen window that backs on to the vegetable garden.

On the fourth and fifth days, when the postbox remained empty, I no longer concerned myself with the events of the novel at all but thought about what could be holding up the arrival of Nishimura's next blue airmail sheet. Perhaps he had made direct contact with Navaz and was sending the final instalments straight to her home address. Perhaps Navaz had noticed my tampering with Nishimura's prose—a fortnight previous, I had sent off a rushed and clumsy page—and was herself circumventing my involvement. On the sixth and seventh days, I did not walk down to the post office but stayed in my rooms reading over those original pages of Nishimura's that I had not sent on to Navaz. After my days of laborious translation, I felt as if I understood the minutiae of Nishimura's style. I found I could anticipate his choice of vocabulary, his turns of phrase, his sentences that curved, brief and poignant, like the span of a bridge, or went on long after you thought now, now they must break off, if not at this phrase then surely at the next. Still, while I could imitate the stuff of Nishimura's writing, what had been eluding me was the shape of the story itself.

In my reduction of the novel to a series of foolscap pages, I had little feeling for Nishimura's handling of his narrative, had not seen the larger picture. Reading the last pages in a single sitting, I noticed how Nishimura made no connection between sections, simply stacked them, like kindling, one against the other. There were gaps also, as if he had not written in the details of events that were elsewhere elliptically suggested. A great deal was made, for instance, of Sanki's asking the maid to the pictures although nothing further is said of this expedition. Similarly, Mr Oliver invites the maid to address him by his first name although it is never revealed what this is. It occured to me then that it would be entirely in keeping with Nishimura's style for this last line, which I had thought signalled the imminent arrival of another blue page as unambiguously as if it had read *to be continued*, to be, in fact, the last line. The next day, the empty postbox confirmed my suspicions, left me with the impossible blank of my days and Sanki, the maid and Mr Oliver, like skydivers in freeze-frame, falling towards each other but who knew what final constellation.

Now the masseuse is asking me to turn over but I refuse. At least, I think of it as a refusal, as having won the upper hand, but I allow myself to be seen as politely declining.

'No, thank you,' I say, 'I only wanted you to make my back.'

Professor Mody gives a little snort from his couch, whether of disappointment or relief it is hard to tell. The woman in white moves to stand beside the professor. She unbuttons his gown, lets it trail like mine on either side and begins to massage his head and neck. I have no intention of watching the professor yet I find myself looking across the gap between our couches with an interest that seems sharper than curiosity. Professor Mody faces the far wall and the back of his neck, usually concealed by the collar of his safari suits, looks soft and unprotected. His body, too, is not what I had expected although I hope it is understood that I had no expectations in this connection. It is brown, of course, but seems tauter, more contained, than I had imagined, than I might have imagined if I had ever given it any thought. It pools out a little, spreading at hips and chest where it touches the vinyl surface of the couch. When the professor's shoulders are pummelled, his buttocks move as if they were filled with water.

I try and guess Professor Mody's age. I have thought of him simply as 'old', years being one more thing that separates him from me. He is, after all, his name plate tells us, the *Retired* Reader in Japanese Literature. Now, with his body laid bare beside me, I think his grey hair and deliberate movements might be deceptive; perhaps he is only in his mid-fifties. I have no confidence in my ability to estimate his age. While I can recognise in someone else all the ages I myself have been, and even ten or fifteen years in advance of that, there is a substantial territory beyond my reach whose signs—a loss of skin elasticity, a dulling of the eye, the veining of the face—I read ineptly. Is Professor Mody older or younger than my father, for example? The professor rolls over inside his gown, lies still again as his face is handled: his cheeks pulled away from his teeth, his eyelids stretched back to reveal the roundness of the eyeball, his ears tugged. His chest is almost hairless, his feet poke up at the ceiling. His penis falls across his thigh; darker than his leg, its bevelled tip has a slight shine.

As Professor Mody's shoulders and chest are massaged, his penis stirs and swells until it sketches an eyebrow's neat curve in the air. The masseuse seems unperturbed by its progress. She moves slowly down his body to where it waits, head raised. Without haste, she works around it, kneading the professor's hips and thighs, then manipulating the skin over the kneecaps, sliding her hands the length of the professor's shins. The professor's erection is not large but sure of itself. The masseuse finishes squeezing his toes in both hands and stands for a moment at the base of the couch. Her hands on the couch remind me of the way that Prakash rested his hands beside him on the seat before beginning our tour of Nandalore. I would be lying if I said there wasn't a certain sense of anticipation. When the masseuse turned and left the room, I felt that anticipation slide unexpectedly from the professor's couch to mine. I remain lying on my belly since to stand up now might be misunderstood as an invitation. Professor Mody makes no move. It is not fear that keeps me here, naked except for the gown beneath me, but a kind of awkward embarrassment. Somehow or other, I find myself in a strange house in an unfamiliar area with a man I barely know, both of us, at a generous estimation, half-clothed, and the man in a state of what my mother once coyly described as 'sexual excitation'. I sense that now is not the time for making appeals to propriety.

The masseuse returns. She holds a soapy cloth and lathers Professor Mody's penis with that blend of admiration and contempt I recognise from the car-wash boys in the courtyard. Through the suds, the professor's penis looks darker still, like wood, the top of a walking stick or a mahoganied baluster. The cloth moves faster and faster although the masseuse remains unmoved, staring out across the room as if she were not attached to that arm, that soapy flannel, that dark root. Professor Mody turns his head to look at me. Sideways, his face looks unfamiliar. His breathing does not quicken exactly but his forehead knits as if he is trying to remember some elusive detail, recall a face. Although my eyes are level with his across the gap between the two couches, I don't think he sees me exactly. Still, I consider it would be gauche to look away. Later, on the landing, as we are following the masseuse downstairs, the professor looks at me, rests a heavy arm on my shoulder and says, 'Call me Mody.'

18

The rickshaw continues the uphill climb. Prakash's voice is pitched over the noise of the engine.

'At the top of this hill is a temple. You will see things here you have never seen before.' I am tired of seeing things never seen before. I would give another one hundred and twenty rupees to see something familiar.

'There is a mango tree growing in the courtyard, planted three and a half thousand years ago. It has four branches, representing the four Vedas. Fruit from one branch tastes different from fruit off another.' Navaz and I are no longer fascinated by the strange, by tombs that birds will not fly over, by marvellous mango trees. We have seen enough. We want to be back at the Hotel Printravel, washing from the big blue buckets, in bed reassuring ourselves of the unmiraculous solidity of our limbs.

Outside the temple, there are several rickshaws and a bus. I recognise one of the drivers from the water mill, the German couple, and some of the Americans from the fort. We exchange the sheepish smiles of the unintroduced. Prakash leads us up the stairs to the temple entrance. He has seen our disloyal smiles in the carpark and is treating us with a measured cruelty. At the foot of the stairs he says, 'Do not give anything to the beggars. They are liars and thieves,' but he walks several steps ahead of us and must know how we are following him, wading uphill with hands and truncated limbs tugging and brushing at our legs. After us come the Americans like an Easter parade, pressing small coins into outstretched hands and bowls which always remain empty, held out for the next coin and the next.

Inside the temple grounds is the mango tree, smaller than I had imagined, its trunk rising from the concrete-hard earth. Sitting against its trunk is an old woman, her legs tucked beneath her as if they too have been growing into the ground for three and a half thousand years. At first I think she is selling shoes, she has so many gathered about her in pairs but, as we walk in, she points at our shoes and clears a space for them among her collection. The Americans have caught up with us. They are slipping off their elastic-sided sneakers and handing them over with another coin. Prakash is at the opposite wall, taking off his black leather shoes, his schoolboy shoes, and leaving them, toes to the wall. He waves us over and Navaz and I limp across, our buckles undone. The old woman has noticed our defection. She begins to shout across the yard to Prakash, who waves one hand at her dismissively, the other at us in a hurry-up.

Our sandals flank Prakash's: we stand in our bare feet. The woman continues to scream, waving her arms over the shoes surrounding her, tossing her head at where our three pairs of shoes stand foolishly on their own. The obedient Americans are standing in their stocking feet, their backs are turned on us, one of them is taking the old woman's picture, as she sways back and forth like a cobra, a shoe in each hand. Prakash shouts back at her in English for our benefit.

'A temple. This is a temple,' he shouts. 'Not a shop. We come here to pray, not to give our money to some cheating layaround.' Navaz and I are embarrassed now. We hang our heads in a travesty of prayer, our camera hangs, black and heavy, from my hand. Prakash has forgiven us. He puts one hand on each of our shoulders and, on tiptoes, guides us away.

The Americans fall back from us on either side. We slip between them like temple snakes, low and dangerous. Prakash takes us around the various altars, introducing us to the stone-faced deities, their necks hung with flowers, their foreheads and feet coloured with crushed chalk. I am making no attempt to follow the lineages Prakash is outlining for us. I am watching him watching Navaz, his tongue licking at the corner of his lips. He is pleased with us now. He scurries between us like the squirrels Navaz's family have promised us in the grounds of the Taj Mahal, but even when he is at my side his squirrel eyes rarely leave Navaz. I am tired of the whole thing. Suddenly it seems it would be an enormous relief to be with the Americans, who know the safety of the pack, travelling from fort to temple in a tour bus, ever only one face, one pair of mirrored sunglasses, one nametag, among dozens.

99

Prakash, the practised performer, has saved the best for last. At the back of the temple there is a thin corridor opening into the courtyard at both ends. From floor to ceiling both its walls are covered in carvings. Prakash is standing at the entrance of this narrow passageway, smiling, rubbing his hands together. He is giving out dates, accounts of different religious styles, historical information, like a machine.

'All these carvings were finished hundreds of years ago,' he is saying, 'but everything in the world today is already on the walls here.' Over his shoulder the first few feet of wall can be made out: there is a tree with each leaf raised and casting a tiny shadow, some god sits beneath its branches, a small flame sprouting from his head; a man with a monkey head washes his feet in a river, a bird flying overhead drops something into the water beside him.

'You look carefully,' Prakash exhorts us. 'You will find many wonders, the space rocket, the television, the fountain pen.' He waves us past him with the infectious boredom of the spruiker.

None of this impresses me any more. It seems much longer ago than this morning that I was pleased to press a coin on to the whitewashed side of a tomb and have it stay. Now it is clear to me that it is all done with magnets. If there are televisions and roller-skates in here then it is because they have been carved in the last thirty years. It occurs to me now that even the old shoe custodian is probably known to Prakash—his mother, perhaps—and their fight is staged every afternoon to maximise the donations from the other tourists. Navaz is working her way down the outside wall, she is slow and thorough as a mine sweeper. I take the opposite wall and, back to back, we move down the dim corridor towards where Prakash can be seen, through the arch of the doorway, hunkered down in a patch of sun. There is a girl with two upturned bowls, a frog concealed beneath one, and a king choosing the empty bowl with his outstretched finger. There is a man fixing an elephant's head on to the stump of another man's neck, a tree with breasts before which the woodcutter throws down his axe. No television, no satellites: I glance ahead to see if any are coming my way. A man with seven fingers holds his hand up beside his head like some strange fruit. A woman is kneeling on the ground, naked, her hands are behind her, taking the weight of her body, which curves away perfectly like an upturned dinghy. Her wing of oiled hair falls back from her forehead, Navaz's beaked nose rises cleanly from her face. Kneeling before her in the same position, body curved back, hands behind him, is a man. His arms and thighs bulge with muscle, his lick of hair covers one dark eye. His shortness hardly matters now, the thick length of his penis connects the two bodies like an engine coupling.

I hear my heart beat faster and faster like an orange rolling down stairs. I move quickly on to the next carving and the next, past flowers thrown beneath horses' hooves, a dog that wears a turban, bats, fruit, trees. Navaz is somewhere behind me in the tunnel, Prakash is still squatting in the sun, smoking a cigarette now, the sun lighting the halo of smoke around his head. I cannot bring myself to look at him. I hurry to the entrance and find my sandals raked into the huge collection in the shade of the mango tree. I hand over five rupees to Prakash's mother. She looks at me blandly, her upturned face gives no sign that these brown sandals are any more memorable than, say, this pair of blue and white sneakers. I can see no family resemblance. At the top of the stairs I look back and see Navaz and Prakash, their heads together in laughter, standing close, smoking, at the back of the temple enclosure.

19

I saw Lillian in her Captain Oates costume one more time, months after that shoot in the backyard beside the garage. I had not imagined that she would keep the beard but there it was, grey with talcum powder although not splintered with ice. I suppose she was in too much of a hurry to ice the beard. Besides, it had been me who solved the problem of the beard the last time, fastening it, while wet, around a bottle standing in the freezer and spraying it with water every hour for six hours until tiny icicles beaded its thick mat. Now Lillian stood on the front steps, instead of the Antarctic blast, my summer garden her backdrop. It had been a hot day, was still too hot to water, but she stood there, half-way down the stairs, one hand on the railing, looking back up towards me in the doorway and Navaz, sitting between us, on the top step. I had come from the kitchen where I was sterilising some clay planters. It was a strange moment, I hardly need say. Lillian had on the same rubber trousers she wore in the photograph that now hangs in the National Gallery and the hood of her fur-lined anorak was fastened tight around her face. I was wearing her apron and Navaz, whose strange tone had brought me from the kitchen in the first place, was sitting silently between us in that intermediate position I recognised as mine.

Whatever had been drawn from Navaz in that wheedling voice I had hardly recognised as her own, I never knew. Now she sat silent, one eloquent hand reaching out and squeaking a couple of fingers down Lillian's rubberised thigh. I stood in the doorway, feeling as if I had interrupted something, as embarrassed as if I had walked into Lillian and Navaz's bedroom on those nights when the sounds of what I suppose can only be called their lovemaking had me tossing in my single bed or listening, in the dark, from a chair just behind my bedroom door.

Lillian said, 'I may be gone for some time.' The yellow stars of the tomato plants moved in the waves of heat rising from the ground behind her. Her face had a sheen of sweat. It is some measure of her greatness that she did not seem ridiculous. She turned on the stair and moved heavily down the path without a backwards glance. To this day, I am not sure if it was her rubber trousers slowing her down and making her swing her legs heavy and wide or whether, even then, she was miming walking through drifts of snow. Navaz sat for a moment longer, holding her knees in her arms, then she stood and embraced me. There was something formal in her that made me think of the word *embrace*. Even when she had kissed me in the twilight garden, her mouth smoky on mine, she had not held me like this. I gathered her to me, to Lillian's apron. Do not wonder where such confidence comes from: I thought I was comforting her.

We stood there for too long on the front step. I had Navaz in an awkward clasp, her shoulder pushing my chin back against my chest, but neither of us seemed able to move. It was as if we were waiting for some external direction, as when Lillian would arrange us for a photograph, or *shoot* as I learned to say, and call from behind her camera for a hand to be lowered, or a face half-turned against the light. I had my nose to Navaz's cotton shirt which smelled of cigarette smoke and another smell of sun on skin, not unpleasant, like water on metal; I was thinking about what to do next: who knows what Navaz was thinking. I pulled back from our embrace, smiled false encouragement at Navaz, whose face seemed suddenly somehow pale, even young, before me, and led her down the corridor to the kitchen where I imagined a consolatory cup of tea, some exchange of womanly confidences over the table in the afternoon's last slant of light.

This is a moment I often return to now; I rerun my passage from the front porch to the kitchen trying to see if there was something I missed the first, the second, the fifth time around. But instead of turning up forgotten details, my remembered scene gets simpler and simpler, collapsing in on itself until what remains are only the movements and not the emotions, like the black and white footprints of my parents' ballroom dancing charts. I see myself lean back from Navaz, smile nervously. I step back, turn, mount the small doorstep. I see my hand take Navaz's as I lead her towards the kitchen. I am in

Lillian's blue- and white-striped apron; Navaz is a step behind me, our hands sensitive in each other's grasp. Some days I can smell the earthiness of my clay planters. And then it is as if there are some frames missing, burned out in the heat of the projector's bulb, for now it is Navaz who is leading me, who has me by the hand and is guiding me off-course, not to the kitchen, but turning towards me in the doorway of her and Lillian's bedroom.

Perhaps you think, as I sometimes do, that given the importance I attach to memory, or rather, given that memory is the only thing remaining to me, the following scene might be fixed in my mind, might be recalled with the certainty with which I can remember Lillian's work. This does not seem unreasonable yet it is not so. While I can remember nothing of that moment when Navaz's hand in mine became my hand in hers, I am suspicious even of those images I can recall without effort, which come back to me with the force of memory. For didn't I remember for months the shirt Navaz was wearing that day, the shirt I pressed my face against, which I saw Navaz remove carelessly over her head without undoing its buttons, as the green-striped shirt with button-down collar we actually bought in our first fortnight here? And did Navaz really take my head in her hands again, press her lips against my forehead, or am I confusing this kiss with that earlier one in the almost dark of the vegetable garden?

Here is the scene as I recall it. Navaz has me by the hand; she turns to me in the doorway of her bedroom. She is beautiful. Her hair slides across her forehead, her nose curves down to her slight smile: everything slips away like butter melting. Beside her I am, even Lillian is, an ordinary person. Our mouths touch: we kiss. Do not expect further description than this. We kiss. We move into the bedroom. Navaz removes her clothes, not frivolously but easily. I watch her for as long as I can before drawing the heavy curtains, stopping her hand on the light switch. She undresses me in part, unbuttons my shirt, pushes aside my T-shirt, unbuckles my belt. She presses me against the mattress and hovers over me as if I were food. And always—while Navaz's mouth is on mine; her tongue, then teeth, at my nipple; her hand between my legs, not in the slow, then fast, strokes of the science teacher, but actually inside me, knocking the breath from me in muscular thrusts—I am thinking only of Lillian, outside somewhere in the remains of the day, walking the streets in her fur-lined hood and rubber trousers.

20

Professor Mody—or Mody, as he insists I call him now—has taken to calling on me in the evenings. Once he has climbed these five flights of stairs, he is not nearly as assured as he is in his own room with its fountain playing against the back wall. He does not know where to put himself and stands too long in the doorway, awkward. He brings me small gifts—books, mainly, from his own collection—and he crosses the floor towards me with them held out in both hands as if they were divining rods. I have no interest in translating these. I barely glance at them. I keep them for a few days before returning them to the professor. Last week, after Professor Mody has left, I find in his latest offering a postcard inserted between the pages as a bookmark. It is a Japanese woodcut: I suppose it would be called erotic art. It is divided in quarters and its four pictures lead from one to another. The story it tells, or, as Lillian would say, *narrates*, is a simple one. In the first square, a woman kneels on the floor, her head touches her knees, her gown is pushed up to reveal her buttocks. A man kneels before her, his penis, longer than his forearm, curves from a slit in his dress. Her anus is drawn in with precision. It is perfectly round and a little swollen. The second picture is as the first but the man has buried himself half-way in that dark knot. In the third picture he is clothed again, the front of his dress flat and undisturbed. He bends a grateful face to the woman's buttocks which are still bare; the round of his lips mimics that other pursing. In the fourth, they take a cup of tea. The professor is trying to tell me something. I replace the postcard between the same pages and return the book to him a few days later without comment.

Navaz also used to lend me books. I read all of her translations first although she insisted they were not the best books on her shelves. It was more than a politeness on my part: I was trying to find out how something could change while still equalling itself.

Her books were packed so tightly in her shelves that, fetched down, their pages seemed reluctant to open. Spines cracked and each page clung to the next so that reading was a series of small violences. Although it seemed as if each book had never been opened before, indeed, was not even designed to be opened, I would often find signs of someone else having earlier passed this way. It was not simply that one page might be torn slightly or spattered with some dark liquid but that each such desecration was described and dated in Navaz's careful hand. So on page seventy-three of *The Adventures of Peregrine Pickle* a yellowed smear is labelled *Geneva, milk chocolate, 1968,* while against two almost grey crescent shapes, their missing portion making up the full circle, is *20 August, café au lait.* Some of the entries were more elaborate than others: I remember a note in *Little Dorrit* reading *Munich, minestrone (fish base)* and once, just as I was starting to question Nellie Dean's reliability, the accusatory *Indian ink—Lillian.*

The professor's books, of course, are not similarly annotated. Still, I wonder if they aren't also stained with their own marginal stories. Professor Mody visited me recently, just before he brought me the Japanese woodcut, carrying under his arm two books in a paper bag, slim companion volumes printed on rough textured paper. I have no idea what sort of books these are: they could be about anything. Although I have no curiosity about them, I leaf through them looking for something extra, something out of place, beyond the story. Perhaps it is a habit of mine since reading Navaz's books with their running commentaries, this interest in the way people write themselves across their pages. The professor's marks are almost always scholarly: he draws attention to one author's citation of another; he records two possible translations of an ambiguous phrase. These two books have exclamation points in their margins. Without bothering to translate the passages they mark, I can see that they include much of the vocabulary we learned at school from the wall chart titled *Parts of the Body*: knee, mouth, hair. The exclamation points are perfectly vertical, suspended over their dots. I can imagine the professor drawing them in with a careful hand. Towards the end of the second book, two of the pages are stuck together with an unspeakable glue.

I make no attempt to prise them open but replace both books in the paper bag to return to the professor on his next visit.

Perhaps you are wondering what was in all those books Professor Mody was bringing me, were they poetry, philosophical treatises, novels? You have the curiosity that ought to have been mine. Really, I couldn't say. They were books, that is all. It is not that I did not understand that they were the professor's message to me, that he had, as my mother would say, designs on me, or even that I was uninterested in that message. Rather it was that I could read him more easily than I could his books. He was always a gentleman, courteous, proper, and he hung out his signal flags according to the rules. He comes to see me more and more regularly. There is no longer any need for me to call in at his apartment with my enquiries. If I don't see him tonight, I will see him tomorrow. One evening last week, when seven o'clock, his usual visiting hour, had passed, I glanced up from my work to see him loitering at the end of the lane, knocked about by the human traffic pouring down the hill at the end of the day. He looks a little lost, or rather, a little cast down. He watches the buses come down the street and, every now and then, he turns and tilts his face up towards my window on the fifth floor. I knew at once how I would seem in my window, staring across to the street, like a postage stamp, my head dark in a yellow square. After an hour, he turns and walks away.

When Professor Mody visits me, he sits in a chair opposite. He watches me examine the books he has brought and then, because a silence stretches itself between us, he makes conversation: something he has read in that morning's paper perhaps, how Betty is progressing with her Japanese, with her diplomat's son. I do not ignore him exactly. I nod and say, 'No' or 'So' as the occasion requires. Eventually, even Professor Mody runs down and, with a last look over his shoulder, takes the stairs down to the yard. The professor does not know how to pass the time as I, alone in my four rooms, have learned to do. He still thinks time is like money, something to be seized, something to be worked. He thinks of time as something to get through when time, of course, is something which must get through you. Passing time is like excreting something, it is the same *passing* as in *passing a motion*. The secret is to let the day move through you as I imagine water sluices through the gold-panning sieve, the wash of gold always in the next, the next, the next swirl of water.

The days pass and I continue my work. Although no more letters addressed to Navaz arrive, every three days I walk down to the post office as before and post her my latest blue sheet. I am writing Nishimura beyond his own ending. Once I had realised there was to be no further mail from Nishimura, it took me another two days to decide on this course of action. Having chosen to continue with the novel, I sent a page to Navaz that very day before the gap between letters widened too suspiciously. There was no time to finalise anything significant, to move the maid towards either Sanki or Mr Oliver, so I engineered a floating section, a section where little happened except Sanki remembering his mother's face over the edge of his cradle and the smell of her when she took him in his arms. I admit it was a strange piece, with the ruthless logic of a dream. I showed it to Professor Mody when he visited and, after he left, corrected a couple of expressions he had lingered on, puzzled. I pushed it through the slot at the post office and bought myself three days' grace.

The professor is growing restless. He calls on me earlier and earlier. He does not even pretend, as he once did, to be passing by, to be in the area. He hesitates at my door, then walks whatever gift he has brought that day into my apartment at arm's length. He continues to wear his safari suits but they no longer have that authoritative look of the almost uniform. He seems to have shrunk inside them and although he still carries himself upright, there does not seem so much of him to carry. He is losing weight. He is writing me onto his body.

21

Last night I couldn't sleep. I lay awake, first in one bed and then the other, before getting up, sitting out a couple of dark hours in my study. I had been asleep, had been woken by a noise coming through the bedroom wall, the repeated squeal of a mattress spring offset by the low groan of a wooden bed frame. I recognised it immediately—such sweetness, such sadness—and could imagine without difficulty those actions taking place a brick's width from where I lay. I pressed my ear to the cool plaster of the wall but there was nothing other than the creaking of the bed, no gasp or pant, no word moaned on an outgoing breath. Raising myself on my elbows, I ground my belly against the mattress, simulating the movements of the man as he watched for the clenchings and unfurlings of his wife's face in the half light. Then on my back, as the squeaks and groans came closer together, I closed my eyes against his curiosity, yet, still knowing myself to be watched, flared my nostrils with each surge of my hips. In my bed, alone, riding out someone else's pleasure, my self-sufficiency, my containment, regrouped as loneliness. Even in the other bed under the window, nothing could protect me from the dark throw of her hair against the pillow, the tented white sheet where her leg hooked over his, from his shoulders catching the light as they rose and fell. I got up, slipped my feet into sandals, and came to sit here over the dark courtyard.

I am sure it won't surprise you if I say how my memory took me then and shook me till my bones cracked. It had me by the throat, like a dog with a rat, like a 105-degree fever. When I moved into Lillian and Navaz's house, or rather, when I, like a piano, had been moved in there, our routines remained largely unchanged except those regarding our going to bed. While I was still living in my aunt's house across the hedge, it was always me who stood up, early or late, made some comment about how tired I was, how I must be going; it was always me who withdrew, who called an end to the day. For the longest time, the only occasion I had seen Lillian and Navaz making any preparations for bed was the night I met them, the night of the party, when I stole back across the wet lawn to stand in the gap of the hedge and watch the two of them straightening the furniture, collecting plates and glasses, and then their lights going off one by one. After that, I never spied on them like that again, strung between the two houses like a bead on a string. They would stay up until I stood to leave, Lillian would say *Good-night* and walk me to the front door. For the first week or so that I lived with them, this pattern remained the same, except that now when I stood up to go to bed Lillian only led me down the corridor to my room.

Then one night, I remember it was early because I had not yet thought of going to bed, I was talking to Lillian when Navaz put aside her book, stood up, said she was tired, might call it a night. How strange my sentence sounded in her mouth. Lillian ducked her head at me and led Navaz down the corridor to their room opposite mine. I waited for her return but fifteen minutes passed and still I was sitting alone in the front room. I picked up Navaz's book, so that Lillian would not find me unengaged when she came back, taking care to hold it open at the page Navaz had marked. I do not know what language it was in. I could recognise the letters but not the words. I tried to pronounce a few of them aloud: my tongue sounded thick and my voice croaked in the empty room. Perhaps it was half an hour before I realised the house was silent, that Lillian's ducked head meant not *a moment, please* but *goodnight*, and another few minutes before I abandoned my attempt to sit up on my own. I felt my way down the dark corridor, brushed my teeth, slipped into bed without turning on my bedside lamp.

You know how it is when you turn out the lights and feel yourself to be in darkness until the objects in your room show themselves to you one by one, first the line of light leaking from under your curtain, catching the end of your bed, then the white spread of the book on your bedside table, the gleam of the far wall. This was how it was that night as I lay in bed, in a house I had thought of as quiet, as sounds leached through to me, first sketching the lines of, and then revealing fully, some nocturnal scene. The water sang in the pipes for a little longer; the floorboards in the corridor ticked. But there was already another noise, not quite as elaborate as a moan, a kind of creaking despair, that seemed to grow louder as the other sounds faded into the night. I did not know what you already know. I eased myself from my bed, stood in my darkened doorway. For one mad moment I considered waking Lillian and Navaz to see if they knew what it was. The sound increased, took shape, ascended a scale. It sounded like the increasingly confident repetition of a vowel in a foreign tongue. I recognised Lillian's voice, although *recognise* suggests an easy identification I did not manage. I left the door ajar and returned to my restless bed, throwing off my covers one moment, then pulling them around my ears, as if I were running a temperature. Even with my head muffled in my bedclothes, Lillian could be heard without difficulty: she sounded as if she were forcing something or being forced, as if she were giving up something precious.

Then there was silence: my ears buzzed with the house's quietness. I only know I fell asleep because I woke with my door open to the corridor's light, the silhouette of Navaz in my doorway asking me if I wanted a hot drink. I pulled on my dressing-gown and, leaving Navaz in the kitchen, sat on the front porch with Lillian. She also wore her dressing-gown but otherwise she looked exactly as she had when we were talking previously in the front room. She said nothing of her performance and I certainly made no mention of it. We sat there companionably over the garden—I had yet to put in my summer vegetable plot—a light breeze swelling our dressing-gowns, shivering the bougainvillea that climbed the house. A cat ran across the drive. Everything was grey in the fall of light from the streetlamp. Navaz came with three mugs on a tray. I saw her again as the Spanish maid and, in my secret embarrassment, gulped up my first mouthful of milk and brandy before it had cooled. We talked of this and that, I can't remember the details exactly; Navaz smoked a cigarette; we returned to our beds.

Next door are sleeping now. Twenty minutes or so was all it took but I sat another hour at my dark perch over the yard, after the last moan of the spring, the last splintering creak. As I was getting up, feeling for my sandals at the side of the bed, I tried a small worldly joke on myself.

'The international language of love,' I said, my voice strung up by the sounds coming through the wall. It didn't strike me as funny. I moved myself to the other end of the apartment. It seems like long ago that I listened to Lillian and Navaz on those evenings when the two of them left early for bed. I would wait until they had used the bathroom, turned out the light behind their half-open door, before going to my own room where I would get into bed naked, hold myself still and listen to Lillian; it was always Lillian. After the first few times, I would sit in my dressing-gown on a chair just behind my door, head tilted to one side in the dark, as once in my parents' house I would listen to the concert programme with a clumsy reverence, feeling myself to be a crude channel for such beauty. And afterwards there was always the gathering on the front porch, I remember still the smell of hot milk and Navaz's cigarettes, before we would all three fall asleep in the silent house. Here, it is never silent. Even when next door have fallen asleep—they lie, bodies thrown together on the quiet bed—I listen to the night courtyard: the lift rattles empty down its shaft; the night watchmen exchange a few words at the corner; one of the houseboys throws off the sheet he is shrouded in, stands to piss against a far wall.

There is one more story about this apartment and the sound of bodies coming together in the night; about a night when the house-boys couldn't sleep and it was next door's turn to be driven from their bed, to wait it out with cups of tea in the kitchen. There is one more story but it can wait.

22

I thought I saw Lillian today. Prakash, of course, could not be expected to recognise her and Navaz gave nothing away under my hard stare. I was waiting for Prakash and Navaz in the carpark of the temple. All the rickshaws looked the same to me, their black sides and yellow hoods indistinguishable. The two of them appeared at the top of the stairs: I expected them to be enjoying a certain complicity, smoking each other's cigarettes perhaps, or Navaz stopping on the top step, one hand on Prakash's shoulder, as she fastened her sandal. It was gratifying to see then, although I pretended not to look, Navaz hurry down the stairs ahead of Prakash, her sandals in hand, searching for me among the buses and rickshaws. She looked tired, the skin under her eyes as dark as her lips. I wanted her asleep under the torn mosquito net, in one of the Hotel Printravel's three beds, while I kept watch from a nearby chair, a book open and unread in my hand.

'Shall we call it a day?' I ask as she draws near.

'I've seen enough,' she says, which makes me wonder whether she has seen the carving. Prakash trots across the carpark towards us. He is actually rubbing his hands together in anticipation, something I thought only happened in books.

'Now for the caves.' There is a pause, as he looks from Navaz's face to mine, waiting for his excitement to ignite there. I explain that we are tired, must return immediately to our hotel. Prakash takes a step back as if he has been pushed. His smile hangs on his face for a moment longer, fades.

'But, ladies,' he bows a little from the waist, 'one hundred and twenty rupees is the full day. I am no crook, please. The caves are the best on offer.' He is smiling again, turning his empty hands over and back to show that there is no trickery, no deceit.

'It is not a question of money,' I say, and again, 'We are tired.' I cannot recall my recent unease. My hand sketches a throwing motion in the air when I say, 'It is not a question of money.' Navaz is already climbing into the cabin when Prakash takes her roughly and turns her by the shoulder. He seems to have inherited my agitation.

'Your friend is concerned for your safety,' he tells Navaz. He sounds like a fairground fortune teller, unconvincing.

'If I were to harm a hair of your head,' and, ever the literalist, he actually takes a strand of Navaz's hair between his fingers, pulls it taut until the skin above her temple rises in a gentle peak. What would follow his harming a hair of Navaz's head, we never learn. He releases the hair as suddenly as he had taken it up, climbs into the rickshaw after Navaz and me.

The ride back to town is enjoyable. It is mostly downhill and, this time, I know our destination, our large white room with its blue buckets in the bathroom. At the crest of each hill, Prakash turns off the engine and coasts down. The sun is on our faces and, with the engine off, the rickshaw sounds like a bicycle or a scooter, its wheels spin across the surface of the road. Navaz's hand grips the hem of her shirt where it lies, untucked, in her lap as soon she will hold the edge of the bedsheet, its darns rough against her hip. The town is in sight, its pale roads shining like sandpaper, when Prakash stops the rickshaw, begins to roll a slow cigarette. Navaz and I look at each other, lean forward a little. A naked, dusty man steps out from the side of the road. His hair and beard are long and matted; he carries a staff cut from a tree branch. The small puffs of dust that cloud his footsteps as he walks toward us seem to come from him rather than rise up from the road. He is so thoroughly coated that I think *dusty* long before I register *naked*. He is not, it turns out, actually naked. He wears a kind of leather apron that is, I see when he turns, as brown and chapped as his buttocks.

The dusty man raises his stick in greeting at Prakash, stoops to look in at us in the back seat and then stands alongside, as if he were waiting for the lights to change on a city intersection. Prakash, meanwhile, has his eyebrows up and is nodding in a self-congratulatory manner at us over the back of the seat. I look at this wild man—although truly there is nothing wild about him, leaning on his staff beside the rickshaw he is mild-mannered, patient—and recognise Lillian. It is not that the wild man looks like Lillian, you understand; rather I see how Lillian might look like this. Her unforgettable mouth is yellowed with dust which collects, almost orange, at the corners; her skin is lightly buffed with a dark nugget; I can see the line of adhesive behind her ear where her beard meets her hairline. I turn quickly to check Navaz's reaction: it is true that she is looking past me at the wild man but then she takes in the view of the town from her own window with equal interest. Lillian is certainly close enough to this height. I try to catch her eye but the wild man is not to be distracted by impermanence, by things that come and go, he is fixed on a distant horizon. I think I see something familiar here, that kind of hysterical over-authenticating that Lillian favours; the bare feet and staff, not only the long hair but the beard also, the far-off look.

That evening, long ago in another country, when Lillian had left Navaz and me on the front step, taken to the summer streets in Captain Oates's beard and rubber trousers, that evening marked a change in Lillian's dress-ups, or *stagings* as she preferred to have me call them. She explained it all to me one evening while she stuffed miniature sausage casings for that night's cocktail party. She was correcting me, putting me right, but I didn't mind because by then Navaz had held my head in her hands as if it were her own, kissed me on the lips with her open mouth. I nodded occasionally for Lillian but really I was stealing my eyes at Navaz, her finger resting in her open book, her small smile gracing first Lillian, then me, without discrimination.

'Dress-ups,' said Lillian, as if that word, only the moment before in my mouth, were somehow contaminated. 'Dress-ups suggest that someone is concealing themselves within the clothes of another.' I nodded, in case she should look at me. Lillian was warming to her topic and twisting each sausage she made with a new conviction.

'Whereas if we think of these moments as stagings, as being performed in a dramatic space, we foreground at once both the authenticity and the artifice.' I memorised the difference so I wouldn't make the same mistake again. A translator, I thought, is a staging because she produces work that is both real and not-real but a bank teller is only a dress-up since she loses herself when she leaves her home in her yellow and blue uniform for a day's work in the city.

After that evening when I abandoned the sterilising of my clay planters for the unexpected pleasures of Navaz's bed, Lillian's stagings became more frequent, more unexpected: I even want to say, as if they were epileptic fits, more violent. I lay awake for a long time, perhaps the whole night, while Navaz, pillows pushed aside, face directly on the mattress, slept with her thigh thrown across my hips. I think Navaz thought I had fallen asleep but truly, pleasure simply overtook me and I stopped moving. I imagined Lillian in her hooded anorak, her beard powdered grey, moving about the dark city like a vague unease. I saw her lumbering across the unfenced backyards of our neighbours, under their clotheslines, her shadow falling for a moment on a bedroom blind. She would be pulled downhill to that secret city I once inhabited: even now she is buying a drink for my bald tattooist, being eyed across a bar. Sometime in the night, about an hour before it began to grow light, I heard her let herself in at the back door, heard her footfall awkward in the corridor, her anorak brushing her rubber trousers at each step. Without hesitation she let herself into my room opposite, moved about in there for a while and then, if my hearing is any judge, went straight to sleep. She appeared at the breakfast table in my clothes: she rolled my jeans up at the cuff as I did, had chosen my favourite shirt from all those hanging in my wardrobe. She sat at the far end of the table, eating my breakfast of grapefruit and cereal, and cut her eyes at Navaz every now and then, not, I realised, to see what effect this latest staging was having on her but in a faithful impersonation of myself. Imagine the scene. I felt less myself than Lillian and, as usual, Navaz smiled and said nothing.

Lillian turned up every day that week at the bank in disguise. I know she would not have been pleased to know that I thought of her stagings as disguise but in that setting, with my supervisor watching the back of my head from his office, I was having difficulty remembering the theory. She always chose my queue, no matter how short some of the others were, and every day she deposited or withdrew the hundred dollars she had withdrawn or deposited the day before. She was not always easy to pick. It was only when she was right at my counter and I caught her eye that I recognised her for certain. Once, I remember, she appeared as a technician for a telephone company, once as a businesswoman in straight skirt and blazer. Once she modelled herself on one of my aunt's photographs that I had shown her: her hair is grey and styled; she wears a lemon angora jersey. A dozen times a day, I saw her over the heads of my customers, standing at the back of my line in some outlandish costume. She would near the counter and I would realise with a relief that edged on disappointment that it wasn't her, that her visitation was yet to be endured. After this, I see her everywhere, even in that brief space of time we have left her behind: she is the air hostess in business class, half-glimpsed through the curtain at the front of the cabin; in Singapore, before I recognise Navaz in her new white clothes, I think Lillian has followed us; now she stands, brown and almost naked, at the side of a dusty road.

Prakash has rolled half a dozen thin cigarettes. He hands them over to the wild man who threads them through his beard, except one which he allows Prakash to light for him. Then, the cigarette hanging from his lip, smoke trickling from his nose, the wild man goes to stand at the front of the rickshaw. He takes a handful of dust, holds it against his ear for a moment as if it has something to tell him, throws it against the rickshaw's windscreen. He takes a leafy twig from a bush at the side of the road and sweeps this dust away. Prakash starts up the engine and when we drive away, the wild man is standing again at the roadside where he first appeared, the cigarettes showing white through his beard like chicken bones. Prakash is pleased with himself: he drives, looking at us over his shoulder.

'The caves you don't see,' he says. 'But you see the holy man.' Navaz and I say nothing. We do not even smile as we should.

Prakash repeats himself, adding, 'You see the holy man and you take his blessing.' It turns out that this is what the business with the dust and the branch were for: we have been protected against ill-fortune and, it seems, venereal disease, if this is what is meant by diseases of the lower half. We are not nearly grateful enough.

'How long are you here?' Prakash asks. Then, like a travel insurance agent, 'Yes, you are covered for the time of your stay.' I try and think if any of the blessings I know are wordless as this one was. Lillian, with her taste for the photographic still, the choreographed moment, would not be able to effect a linguistic fake. Yet what are the logistics of her travelling to this country, let alone making contact with Prakash, intercepting our rickshaw?

23

It is much more difficult to write Nishimura's novel from scratch than to change a phrase, or add a sentence, here or there as I had been doing. It is not only that I must come up with a certain amount of narrative development every three days but that, having determined the plot line, I must write it out without fault. My Japanese is a schoolgirl's Japanese: it does not always move in the direction I intend. Professor Mody is a help to me in these matters. He reads my manuscript a couple of times and anything he hesitates over, saying, 'This must be a colloquial expression,' I rewrite before putting in the post. If the professor is puzzled by this sudden turn in Nishimura's phrasing, his new favouring of an informal, street language, he says nothing of it. I read my Japanese phrasebook in bed at night as closely as if it were a novel, finding in its alphabetical listings an engaging enough story: *bring about the end, bring home the bacon, bring up the rear.* I am always casting about for ways in which Mr Oliver, the maid and Sanki will make their intentions visible. I certainly do not mistake these characters for my friends, as I believe some writers do. Perhaps they are Nishimura's friends, even Navaz's, but they are not mine. To me, they are as thin as a piece of paper and as easy to misplace. Sometimes I forget how they talk or even what they look like in the space of time it takes me to pass down the corridor to the bathroom or make a cup of tea in the kitchen.

There is a film I saw once with Navaz that I think Sanki and the maid should see together. I manage to get through the invitation without too much trouble but when I try and write in even the sketchiest details of the film itself my vocabulary fails me: I do not know how to say, *a compromising situation; six of one, half a dozen of the other.* I am forced to rewrite this section. Remembering my schoolday vocabulary drills, I have Sanki and the maid attend the morning market where the apples, the cheeses, the cantaloupes, the honey, the grains, the meat pierced through by the butcher's hook, speak obliquely of their secret desires.

I see how my style, if it can be called that, is not unlike Nishimura's own. Being unable always to take the direct route, I tell everything slant. I leave much unwritten, try to convey the necessary tone through some simpler figuration: Mr Oliver's figure in the doorway, the fall of evening's light. Sometimes, for authenticity, I recycle Nishimura's phrasing so that, in his account, the upstairs floor of the boarding house and, in mine, Sanki's face behind sunglasses are both *moled with light*. In the early part of the novel, Mr Oliver describes the maid as being *innocent as an egg*, a description the maid later uses of Sanki. I read a page of Nishimura before I write anything myself and, when I watch Professor Mody reading over my work, I imagine Navaz's more knowing eye grazing these same lines.

One afternoon, the professor calls on me. Only that morning I have posted my latest airmail letter to Navaz: time, as Sanki will say to Mr Oliver in an upstairs room while the maid deliberates below, weighs heavy on my hands. I answer the door with my sunglasses on, a light jacket pulled across my shoulders. It is not possible for Professor Mody to seem more hesitant than usual but, as he stands in my door warding me off with the book he has brought me, his eyes flick from glasses to jacket to glasses again. I make no effort to take his present from him, or even to move out of his way.

'We are going out,' I say. He impersonates calm, nods as if he had expected as much. On the way downstairs, I see his veined hands tremble under the weight of his gift. I am, of course, calling the professor's bluff. I have no idea where we are going. I wait for him to ask but he seems content to move in my slipstream, at my pace, one step behind.

On the street, I hail a taxi.

'Drive,' I say to the man behind the wheel. To the professor, I say nothing. The driver has seen too many American movies. He accelerates away from the curb, turns immediately into a sidestreet, then another, reverses down a one-way lane, as if we are being pursued. When he has a moment, he catches my eye in the rear-vision mirror, says, 'I am driving. I am driving.' From my window,

I recognise an eating house at which Navaz and I once lunched. Although we have been driving for some time, it is only two minutes walk from my door.

'Stop,' I say to the driver. He brakes immediately, shrugs at the meter. I get out of the taxi. The professor follows.

He has left his book on the back seat, is looking about as if he has never stood on this street before, although it lies between my apartment and his. I stare at him from behind my sunglasses. He recollects himself: he pats the pockets of his safari suit, hands a note through the window to the driver who offers no change but, holding the money between his teeth, wrenches the car into gear and is away. Professor Mody looks down at his empty hands as if they were gloves. I see him remember his book but he bites his lip, says nothing. Inside, I order plates of cheese, *pav bhaji*, jelly and ice cream, a pot of tea. I chat pleasantly with the professor: 'You are well?' I ask and, 'How are things with you?' Our little meal comes to a close. I stand to leave. The professor is embarrassed. He speaks in a low voice without looking at me.

'I have no money,' he says. 'That fellow took my last hundred.' I incline my head at him politely.

'I will walk home,' I say. 'Perhaps I will see you tomorrow?' On the street, I do not turn: I do not see the professor handing over his watch to the manager, walking to his bank, his shadow short in the full sun.

24

I woke this morning with some lines of poetry on my mind. It is as if I have been woken by their recitation: I think I can hear their last resonances just this side of sleep. At first, I feel that I have made them up myself, that they are for the novel. I roll to face the wall, try to work out whether I can translate them, the context in which they might be said. *I dream of journeys repeatedly: / Of flying like a bat deep into a narrowing tunnel, / Of driving alone, without luggage.* I think it is Mr Oliver who would say this. It is least like him and will indicate his agitation. I do not know the word for *bat*; if it is not in my dictionary, could I use *bird* instead? There is something less proper—hence, in this context, more appropriate—about a bird, rather than a bat, flying into the dark, the tips of its wings brushing closer and closer the damp rock. It is only when I think of changing the wording that I realise it is not mine to change; remember learning the piece at school, the whole class chanting the lines with an almost religious steadiness.

Besides, my dream was about a ship. It was a dream about myself and the professor and, if I tell you about it now, it is not because I think it says something better than I am able but because there was a pleasure to be had in it that did not fade with waking. The professor was the captain of a ship that was something of a cargo ship, something of a cruise liner. In the dream, there seemed nothing strange about this. He invited me to travel with him as his guest. He was a figure of confidence, his safari suit now white with nautical trimmings, a flat white cap on his head. We walked into our cabin, a very generous shipboard space, and the professor—or the captain, as I suppose I should now call him—laughed, said with indulgence, 'I see they've put our bed on the diagonal.' The significance of this was not clear to me but certainly the bed was angled away from the wall. We were not, as in the poem, without luggage although we were travelling lightly, the captain with a canvas duffel bag, me with a leather case. The captain settled me in before taking his leave. There were things beyond this hotel-like bedroom that demanded his attention. I had no clear understanding of what these might be but I imagined nets of cargo swung up into the sun on the end of a crane's arm; boiler rooms ticking over in the guts of the ship; a crew with an untempered loyalty that broke and rolled like mercury.

Left to myself, I lay across the bed, reading the book I had brought with me, a historian's account of the opening of these sea passages reconstructed from ships' logs. Through the wall came squeaking and scratching sounds which I explained to myself as the winching into the hold of cargo. I imagined a cross-section of the ship and did not feel reassured by this cabin's small square of light suspended over the battened-down depths of the hold. What was it exactly that we were transporting? For the first time, I wondered if we would be in any danger. I laid aside my book, whose discussion of slave routes, maritime discipline and medical records was no consolation to me. The captain still had not returned from whatever tasks were engaging him. I saw the ship as it would be in a few days, far out to sea, no land visible in any direction, and the storm I then worked up spared itself no Hollywood excess: driving rain, waves like three-storey buildings, a tense scene in the engine room. I couldn't remember whether the ship had masts or not—my dream seemed to be entirely played out within the confines of the cabin—but nevertheless I had them splintering, pitching into the sea, skewing the ship on its side.

The captain would be as he always was, gallant, courteous, even affectionate. He hands me the life preserver, a white ring with a red cross painted on it, and speaks into the camera, bravely, beautifully, of his love for me. He does not actually say *love* but it is there in the water coursing down his face like tears, in the force of the wind that wrenches the words from his mouth. I stand beside him with my life preserver which may as well be a brick for all the practical assistance it lends me. In the one moment, I realise that I love the captain as I have never loved anyone before; that it is the most useless love in the world being absolutely without future. What good to me are these last words of the captain when the wind blows the water white and black, when the salt water that even now pulls at our calves, knees, thighs, will soon fill our mouths and float us, together or apart, in the chambers of the sea?

The captain returns to our cabin from whatever winchings and tabulatings, whatever orderings and reorderings, have taken him from my side. He is clean and dry, he carries his cap in his hand: he is in control.

'Don't let me forget to fill in the log,' he says as if it were some small domesticity, rubbish to be put out, a key left for a serviceman. I can match his easy ways. I push away my book, still lying open beside me, and any fading thought of disaster.

'What is it exactly that we are transporting?' I say *we* as though I also have been on deck, supervising the loading of the ship, checking cogs and belts in the engine room.

'Rice,' says the captain. 'Rice and bales of cotton mainly.' There is a frantic screaming, urgent and energetic, through the wall. I am being so studiedly casual that I do not start.

'What is that?' I ask the captain, who is twirling his cap on his index finger.

'It is the guinea pigs,' he explains. 'We have also two thousand guinea pigs. They do not like heights.' The captain's arm mimes the height of the crane at its fullest extent; his eyes bulge as I suppose he would have me believe the guinea pigs' do. I smile, I almost laugh, with relief.

'What do we have guinea pigs for?' I say just to make conversation, for the captain has put his cap aside, is moving towards the bed with insidious intent.

'For their flesh.'

And yet it is not this sentence but that other which still sounds in my room when I wake, *of driving alone, without luggage,* which hangs in the air, almost imperceptible, like a wisp of smoke seen through the telescopic sights of a sniper.

25

Back at the Hotel Printravel, I ring for hot water, undress Navaz in the bathroom and soap her body. My hand is wrapped in a flannel and I wash her ears, the back of her neck, her collar bones: my hand moves under her arms, between her legs. There is no desire in me as I run my flanneled hand over her body or if there is, it is a desire bent double, turned back on itself; a desire to recognise Navaz's boundaries, where the air meets her skin, not to confuse her body with mine. I kneel in front of her and wash each foot, raised in turn, Navaz balancing herself with one hand on my shoulder. I mix the hot water with cold in one of the blue buckets and ladle it over her, washing the soap away, rinsing her hair until it sticks flat to her forehead. She stands there, wet, head a little low with tiredness. Is it her tan skin or the unfaultable line of her body that makes it seem as if she is never naked? Always, she has the certainty of the clothed. Against the plane of her back, the curve of her stomach, its line of hair ascending to her belly button, my own arm, pale yet mottled with heat, looks faintly diseased.

I dry her then. She is letting me take care of her. I take her head in my hands, remembering how once she did the same for me, and towel her hair. She slips into the middle bed, one shoulder hunched high, one hand dark where it holds the hem of the sheet. Through the torn gauze of the mosquito netting, she looks out of focus, blurred at her edges. I sit opposite in a chair, the other beds being too soft to sit on, one of Navaz's books open in my lap. Navaz has pushed her pillow to one side, her hair is damp against her head. Every now and then, she opens her eyes, finds me on the chair, closes them again. She sleeps. I match my breathing to hers, take long breaths in and out as her shoulder rises and falls. I feel more connected to her mouth, slightly open to the mattress, than if I had pressed my own against it.

When she has been sleeping for some time, I begin writing my postcard to Prakash. I head up with the date and write *Dear Prakash* in a firm hand. The postcard I use is one I brought from home after reading a guide book that advised, *Cards and stamps of your own country make a pretty thank you and, in many cases, are more acceptable than money.* The picture on the postcard looks like the surface of the moon, grey whorls crater the entire card: the caption on the reverse reads, *Rotorua—City of Contrasts! Take a break from shopping and visit our Thermal Wonderland where you can see the locals cook and wash in their traditional way!* I try and think whether, since arriving here, anything has proved more acceptable than money. *Dear Prakash,* I write, *We are unable to take up your offer of a further tour of the caves at discount rates. We have both been afflicted with unexpected diseases of the lower half. Please look us up if you are ever in Australia.* I sign it *Helena and Navaz,* pleased with how elegant my name looks when shadowed by Navaz's.

I wash in the almost cold water and put myself to bed behind Navaz, in the bed against the wall, where I can watch her but she cannot see me. Her hair is almost dry now, the shape she makes under the sheet has me on the verge of tears. Perhaps when she wakes we will go down the street for something to eat. Tomorrow, I think, we will cash in our plane tickets and take the day train back to the city or we will catch a bus out to the caves and fly home later that evening as arranged. We can only stay away one night because Navaz must be back in time for Nishimura's next instalment, due the following day. As often as I take Navaz away from the city, from her aunt and cousins and our two single beds separated by the width of their bedside table, I must have her back two days later, to our apartment ten minutes' walk from the post office and her private mailbox. The only time this routine was broken was when Navaz became ill while we were away. I was too frightened to move her or, at least, this is what I said when she recovered enough to know she had been out of the city for over a week. *Frightened* does not describe how I felt tending Navaz, running an ice cube around her dry lips and into the open neck of her shirt, her head dry and hot under my hand while she, delirious, talked to me, to Lillian, of stories she had read or things that had happened to her, I couldn't tell the difference.

So: I am forever consulting maps and timetables, spiriting Navaz away for a weekend at a nearby hill station, for a morning flight to Delhi and a stopover in Agra on the return journey. Navaz would be as happy to stay at our apartment. I do not mean that she resents my moving her about in these short bursts but that she does not prefer one thing over another. If we wake up in strange beds, the morning light seeming to enter the room from the wrong angle, our heads where our feet should be, Navaz rises in a good humour, listens to my plans over breakfast, lets herself be shown the sun temple, the bird sanctuary, the royal art collection. Yet if we wake five flights above the courtyard, Navaz seems as content. She has a shower before the water is turned off—I hear her singing one of Lillian's songs, *my baby thinks she's a train*—waits for me at the table in her dressing gown, smoking the first cigarette of the morning, while I fetch the paper and breakfast from the American Express bakery. All this compliancy is bordered about with her one non-negotiable requirement: every third day she must be back in the city, checking her mailbox for a letter from Nishimura.

It does not escape me that now it is Professor Mody who must deform himself to fit in with this three-day cycle which continues to tick over independently of Nishimura; that now it is Navaz who waits on me, who measures out her life as I measure out mine, with the translation of arrival and dispatch. After finding himself unable to pay for our lunch, the professor does not visit me for a few days despite my invitation: *Perhaps I will see you tomorrow?* He cannot stay away entirely: I see him loitering at the end of the lane most evenings but he does not come up to see me. I wonder if he imagines himself to be inconspicuous, his distinctively set spine and pale safari suits unremarkable from my window. On the fourth evening, just before it gets properly dark, he is approached by a child, from this distance I cannot see if it is a girl or boy. At first he ignores her—surely it is a girl, she is so slight—but she stands her ground, seeming almost to catch the light from the professor's white suit. She wears some piece of cloth about her hips, carries a thick whip twice her length. She beats herself with it: the whip wraps around her body several times; its crack, savage as an axe fall, carrying to my window a second later. The whip cracks twice more. Something, I think it must be her blood, spurts across the professor's chin, the double-breasted front of his jacket. Professor Mody puts his hand to his chin, as if in thought. He looks up at the bright square of my study but, wanting to watch unobserved, I am standing, unlit, at the kitchen window. He takes something from his pocket, hands it to the girl, walks quickly into the courtyard, keeping to the shadows near the walls.

26

I see that I described my dream of Professor Mody and his ship as giving me a certain pleasure on waking. Yet in my account of that dream, there is nothing easily identified as pleasant: the possibility of a storm and the disturbing off-stage of the unplumbed hold where guinea pigs squeal in anticipation of being flesh. It seems to me that the dream is the gold standard of solitude, not simply because you dream alone but because, on waking, the stuff of the dream is uncommunicable. How many times have you woken in bed with someone, cut across their account of the night's dreaming, or waited unlistening, until you might put your own dreams to them? Every dream has a certain tone which the dreamer is unable, although desperate, to recreate: like the sound of a dog whistle, it is pitched higher than human hearing. This is why there is a compulsion to relate our own dreams, a reluctance to hear anyone else's: we prefer our solitude shared; we don't care to share another's. It occurs to me that my story is like a dream, interesting, intelligible, only to myself.

This is not always the way with stories, whatever I say of dreams. Nishimura's story, for example, has a wider appeal; it is not simply something he is telling himself. His story has a certain impetus that allows it to continue being written even after it has finished. I followed it eagerly enough, when my interest in it was a good deal more casual than now, on those evenings when Navaz would read to me. Even the professor was taken by its narrative, although lately he looks at me more searchingly than at those sheets of blue airmail paper I offer up to his inspection. I am having trouble with Nishimura's story, I don't mind telling you. I have decided that it is easier to read than to write. As a reader, I have only to fashion myself to the shape of each page, letting my hand go before my eye, measuring, by thickness, the number of pages to follow; as a writer, I am on my own, up against the face, double-testing each word to see if it is lode-bearing. I seem unable to advance Nishimura's story beyond the geometry of what Nabokov calls *the banal triangle of tragedy*. Sanki has spoken with Mr Oliver; Mr Oliver has spoken with the maid, who, this late in the piece, I have gifted with the name Beatrice; the maid has reported Mr Oliver's conversation to Sanki. I have in my mind now a more ambitious section in which the three of them sit down together, but can't think what occasion might effect this. My study of other novels tells me that a shared meal would be the obvious choice but, at the boarding house, all the tenants eat together, Mr Oliver watches them but does not himself eat and Beatrice doesn't even sit down but moves from kitchen to table, serving food.

This is how I solve my problem. I have the three of them play a board game one night after the evening meal. The other boys have gone to their rooms or out for the night. Mr Oliver, still sitting at the head of the table, sets up the game and invites Sanki to play. Beatrice comes to stand beside them. She is holding a dishcloth and one strand of her hair, damp with sweat or the steam rising from the sink, curls away from her head. Mr Oliver looks at her and lays out three places at the board. At first I had thought the best game for them to play would be chess with its black and white pieces, its logic unfurling at several removes. Still, that returned me to my old impasse: while two played one must look on. Cards, then, held a certain attraction. All three could sit around the table, playing close to their chests, raising their bids and calling each other's bluff. There is an intelligible vocabulary to the card game, where the queen is thrown down and scooped up, where the value of individual cards rises and falls from hand to hand. I do not know how to say *royal flush* however, or what the jack is called and since I cannot ask the professor, who lurks at the end of the lane but does not come up to see me, I settle for the literal eloquence of a word game.

Mr Oliver, at the head of the table, has the board up his way: Sanki sits at his left hand, Beatrice at his right. Beatrice spills the tiles on to the table and arranges them all face down. Each of them selects seven tiles, racks them up in front of them. Sanki draws the highest tile and begins. He makes a solid start with *linnet*. The game is in English, of course. For once, Sanki, Mr Oliver and the maid are already in translation. Sanki does not score highly with his opening move but he almost clears his rack, can choose six new letters. Beatrice and Mr Oliver watch Sanki's hand move among the upturned tiles; they raise their eyes to look at each other while his tiles are being selected. There is a watchfulness to this game that does not follow from a fear of being cheated. There is a pleasure in looking: in being looked at, in being allowed to look. The back of Sanki's head has been seen many times, those darker folds at the back of his neck, as he bends over his garden, and the maid is often caught in the yellow square of the window as she moves between table and sink, but who has seen the way Sanki sticks out his bottom lip when he is thinking; who knows how Mr Oliver puts his hand inside his own shirt, rubs his shoulder, while he watches Beatrice's face fixed on the boy's opposite?

The three of them do not write themselves out too plainly. The tiles I give them do not allow the spelling of *hope* and *desire* or those cruder words which I suspect are not even permitted on the game's board. Beatrice uses the last letter of Sanki's *linnet* for her *gate*; Mr Oliver balances this, taking Sanki's first letter for *walk*. Beatrice turns out to have been one of those children who read the dictionary for pleasure: against the *skirt* and *embark* of the two men, she plays *jauk* and *crissum*, twice she empties her rack with *petechia* and *arbuscle*. They cannibalise each other: Sanki adds *lych* to the maid's *gate*; Mr Oliver puts *corpse* before Sanki's *candle*, beginning a dispute which is only settled with recourse to the dictionary. The dictionary is one of Mr Oliver's. It has speckled endpapers and small half-crescents cut out of the pages where the letters are marked in alphabetically. It is an illustrated dictionary with pictures of an otter and four different kinds of buoy: the can, the nun, the spar and the whistling buoy. Beatrice seems still to find some pleasure in dictionaries. She leafs through the thin pages, she reads out the entry under her name: *A Florentine woman immortalised in Dante's* Vita Nuova *and* Divina Commedia; *the witty heroine in Shakespeare's* Much Ado About Nothing. She finds nothing under Sanki's name or Mr Oliver's, whose first name is still not disclosed to the reader, although I let it be known that alphabetically it falls between Beatrice and Sanki. Once Mr Oliver can make no word with the tiles on his rack and must forfeit his turn.

This may well be my most awkward piece of writing. It occurs to me that what is atmospheric in the cinema might seem stilted when written. It is difficult to convey the mechanisms of an ambiguous glance: the way a room darkens, the windows and the board, its tiles shining like teeth, picked out in the last light. My limited vocabulary is not making it any easier. I have taken to writing out my pivotal phrases in English, translating them only when my course is roughly charted. I want the written equivalent of a pan, its easy shift from face to face without the clumsy connection of *and* or *then*. I would draw the gaze up from that board, that hemmed-in space, reveal without a word the darkness beginning to thicken at the players' backs, to soak up their legs under the table. Clumped at the head of the refectory table, its length stretching away from them like a diving board, I imagine Beatrice, Mr Oliver and Sanki as characters in a scene from one of my late-night, foreign-language films. They do not speak to each other, or rather, they do not say anything consequential. If their fingers touch over the tiles upturned beside the board or one anonymous leg brushes against another, each face in view above the table, looking but giving nothing away, then that is part of the game. They pronounce the words the others lay down; they offer definitions, *it's like the spots in chicken pox*.

When there is the sound of something heavy being put down in one of the upstairs bedrooms, all three look at the ceiling and Beatrice says, 'That'll be Roger.' There is a sense of satisfaction, which I do not know if I convey, in their being together while elsewhere others are heard moving through the ordinariness of their rituals as the day comes to a close. Sanki imagines Roger overhead, hanging his clothes for tomorrow over the back of his chair, examining the collar of his shirt to see whether it will manage another day before going to the laundry. Another boy passes his open door, a towel over his shoulder, on his way to the bathroom. The book Roger was reading at the dining table is open, a few pages on; it lies on the floor beside his bed. Roger cannot make up his mind about the shirt:

he holds it as around an imagined neck and scrutinises it at arm's length. He has no sense that downstairs, under his feet, Sanki still sits in the dining room, playing his tiles, pushing them up against those already on the board and listening for the satisfying clink of their connection.

Beatrice plays her last tiles, *juga*. She puts down two high-scoring letters whose retention would have penalised her in the final account. Neither Sanki nor Mr Oliver have heard of the word but they no longer allow Beatrice the pleasure of explanation.

'Is it not enough that she thrashes us?' Mr Oliver had said, as if to Sanki but all the time smiling across the table to where the maid hangs her head in a touching gesture of delight. Now Mr Oliver's hand creeps to his dictionary: *juga—plural—a pair of the opposite leaflets of a pinnate leaf.* Faking sneakiness, he shows the entry to Sanki. Later that night Sanki will attempt to anatomise his happiness at that moment. He lets his mind go blank as he does when, revising for his examinations, he must recall how the musculature overlays the skeletal system: he traces that happiness backwards like an artery to see whether its source is the closeness of Mr Oliver's head to his own over the pages of the dictionary or the wash of false modesty that colours Beatrice's cheeks. Beatrice too—and possibly Mr Oliver also—is drawing on some doubled bank of pleasure which, despite her apparent ease with words, she cannot name. She looks at Sanki and Mr Oliver bent over the dictionary's opened page, hardly able to make out its small print in the remaining light. Sanki's head on its slender neck reminds her impossibly of a tulip; she sees how Mr Oliver is something else altogether, more organic and—since she is queen of the words—more lapidary. And some sense of queenliness does overtake her then: she looks across at Sanki and Mr Oliver, who have finally finished with the dictionary and are only leaning on it now, shaking their heads and laughing at each other. She looks across at them as if they were her subjects, as if they were subject to her. *She will choose the one who is least like her.*

27

There is no chance for me to check my latest piece with the professor. On the third day he has still not come up to see me although each night I see him at the end of the lane, being pulled in and out of the entrance to the courtyard like a boat moored just beyond the harbour's mouth. I am not sure whether I have *skeletal system* right or the names of the different buoys but I cannot wait for the professor who seems to be waiting for something else. On the third day I type out the page on airmail paper and post it to Navaz. Something stops me from calling in on Professor Mody as I once did, from ringing his bell one evening, climbing his stairs with a twist of hot nuts to have with our beer. For one thing, he would no longer need to spend the evenings down below on the street, unable to come up and see me on the fifth floor, unable to return to his own rooms while my windows are still lit and there is the possibility that I will pass them one more time before bed; for another, to get to his apartment I would have to walk past him as he hung in a doorway at the end of the lane. As it is, I have him before me most evenings, visible, at a certain distance, like a dog on a lead.

The night after I have been to the post office, Professor Mody walks up the lane to my building, keeping close to the shadows near the walls. I see him every now and then as he crosses the fall of light from a high window or hangs for a moment in the double beams of a car's headlights. When he reaches the open square of the courtyard he hesitates, looks up to the empty brightness of my study window. He does not see me standing, watching, two windows along in the dark kitchen. He enters the courtyard as if it were a swimming pool, slides in at the far end, pauses, makes for the side with jerky strokes. From my window I cannot see his face: his head is down, bent over the stain on the front of his double-breasted jacket, and he carries his hand before him like an unexploded grenade. I watch him walk towards me until, face against the cool pane of glass, I lose sight of him entering the building. Four or five excruciating minutes pass like the tedious real time of avant-garde cinema. I throw down today's newspaper on the chair in my study as if it has just been cast aside. If I had not been expecting the professor's knock, so slight it is more like a scratch, I might have missed it. When I open my door, he is standing there as if about to take a curtain call, poised and slightly bent at the waist. His face and jacket, his awkwardly held hand, are spattered with blood. I am surprised that there is, for me, a simple pleasure in seeing him. I would not say I have missed the professor exactly since, like some ridiculous balloon, he has been hovering near me most evenings, but he seems better viewed in my doorway than across the darkening space of the courtyard. I think perhaps I might touch my hand or lips to his cheek if it were not a little slick with blood, if he seemed a little less fragile.

I am not sure what to say to Professor Mody, who stands silent before me, holding out his hand as if it had an eloquence that surpassed words. In the centre of his palm are a few drops of blood which he seems anxious not to lose. I try to remember the protocol of the situation. For half a week I have not seen Professor Mody officially and, when he turns up at my door, he is splashed with blood. Still, I know that the blood is not actually his and anyway, despite being daubed on face, hand and chest as if for an amateur theatrical, there is not much of it. I decide to be welcoming but not over solicitous.

'Won't you come in?' I ask, satisfying myself with the negative framing of this invitation. Then, as if seeing him properly in the light of my apartment, I give a little start, exclaim, 'What happened?'

One hand to my lips, the other rising to my heart, it is me who should be in an amateur theatrical. The professor matches my excess. He allows his knees a momentary buckle, says, 'I was set upon by hooligans. Crack! Crack! Crack!'

At these last three words, he chops his hand about his head, making me uncertain whether this performance recreates the attack or his spirited defence. The drops of blood fly from his hand like mercury, leaving his palm unmarked. We both look at its blankness a moment before the professor raises it to his cheek, brings it down lightly smeared.

'Let me take care of that,' I say, although now Professor Mody's cheek is almost wiped clean. I take the professor by his good hand and lead him towards my bathroom. He comes quietly, sags against the handbasin. I catch myself almost believing his story, see what an easy target he would make on the street. I clean his hand and face; get him to hold a washcloth against his chin; unbutton his jacket and rub its stain with soap. I check the pockets before soaking it in the sink. In the left hand chest pocket, there is a roll of banknotes in a rubberband. It reminds me of the wads of hundred dollar bills I used to handle when I was a bankteller. How far away that other life seems now and yet, as if it were my destination not my point of departure, it is always before me.

'You are lucky to have this still,' I say to the professor, rolling the money between my fingers. He looks at me blankly, as if he has missed a cue.

'The hooligans,' I prompt.

'O yes,' says Professor Mody without much interest. 'Crack, crack, crack.'

Once he sees his jacket immersed in my sink, the professor starts to assert himself again. He no longer droops against the washbasin but eyes himself in the mirror over the sink. Since he has lost weight, the professor's skin is not as taut as it was. He is a little softer now; he has grown breasts. As if that little amount of blood could have soaked through to his skin, I dip my facecloth in the basin and wash Professor Mody's chest. At first I dab politely, almost apologetically, at him but when he stops looking at himself in the mirror, catches my reflected eye, I circle his nipple more purposefully. He raises his hand to his chin as if to staunch some unseen flow of blood, says, 'Perhaps I should go to bed.'

I have to say I consider the bedroom for a moment, its two single beds separated by the bedside table, but it is not the setting I had imagined.

'Shall I call you a taxi?' I stop circling the facecloth on the professor's chest and allow my voice to be inflected with concern.

'No, no,' says Professor Mody. He does not have the effrontery to go on. He holds my eye for a little longer before saying, 'I will sit in your study and collect myself.' The way he says it, it sounds like a question. In a kind of mimed consent, I empty the sink, begin wringing out his jacket. The professor limps away. When I have hung up his jacket to dry, I join the professor in the study: he is sitting in my chair, one of the books he has loaned me open on his lap.

'What are you making of Yukio?' he asks. 'If you need any help with the translation . . .'

I had not realised this was another of Yukio's collections.

'I have not read him,' I say firmly. 'Nishimura is taking up all my time.'

I see that the professor is about to read me another of Yukio's poems. He does not stand up but pins his shoulders back, takes a preparatory breath.

I cannot allow a half-clothed, breasted man to recite erotic verse in my study. I hurry down to my bedroom, leaving Professor Mody in the study, chest inflated, lips puckered in expectation of Yukio's first word. While I am looking in my wardrobe for something to cover the professor's monstrous nudity, I imagine him as I left him, round as a puffer-fish, on an indrawn breath. None of my clothes look big enough for Professor Mody. Even with the weight he has lost, he is still broader than me across the chest and shoulder. There is a loose muslin kurta without a collar that might do or a green shirt of Navaz's, left behind because it had not been washed. I catch myself standing in front of the mirror, holding one and then the other against me, trying to substitute the professor's hair and skin for mine, as I decide which would better suit him. I settle on the green shirt or rather, knowing that it is absurd for me to be selecting a shirt for the professor in anything but a purely pragmatic register, I push the nearest one back into my wardrobe and take the other to the study.

Far from being as I left him, book at the ready, the professor has unearthed from the papers on my desk the photograph taken of Navaz and me on the morning of our departure. He is on his feet and bends over the desk, pinning the photograph to the desktop with the thumb and index finger of each hand. The tip of his tongue is caught between his teeth and he holds the photograph down on the desk as carefully as if he were preparing a cross-section for a laboratory slide. He has an air about him, a kind of triumphant despair, like the detective in a mystery thriller who knows at last and with certainty who the murderer is but only as that man advances upon him, weapon drawn. When he sees me watching him from the doorway, the professor backs away from the desk, takes his place again in my chair. I hand him the shirt and take his place over the photograph.

No doubt, Professor Mody recognises Navaz from the photograph he has shown me of her opposite Nishimura on the back of his copy of *Skin Behind Bone*. She wears, after all, an open-necked pale shirt similar to the one on that dust jacket, her smile so small it is all in her eyes. I have always been fond of this picture of Navaz and me, the little remaining distance between us marked out by a letterbox whose address we are soon to leave behind. Now I see for the first time how Navaz and I are not equivalently placed on either side of the letterbox; how, while I look straight into the camera lens, Navaz's gaze is downcast and left of centre. It hardly seems the same photograph as I remember for here her hand strokes the top of the letterbox as if she cannot bear to leave. I want to go on looking at the photograph, to see whether a closer examination might uncover that picture I once saw there, Navaz and me flanking the letterbox which marks the first stop of the journey even now unravelling from our feet like a map. I promise myself I will look at it later for now the professor has Navaz's shirt on, is trying to decide whether or not to tuck it into his trousers.

The shirt is hardly flattering, in or out. It is too small. Between every button it gapes open to reveal the professor's skin and is so tight across his waist that it corrugates the soft flesh of his belly. Nevertheless Professor Mody looks pleased with himself. He thinks he is wearing my clothes. He is not exactly preening but he cocks his head at his tightly sausaged arms and smiles a little. It is not entirely unpleasant to see the professor's new breasts flattened against the material of Navaz's shirt. Perhaps it is because, long before I met him,

I first saw the professor in a safari suit that now he looks so ridiculous to me in anything else. It is not only that the shirt is too small: it is not the right colour, its sleeves are too short, it is unstructured by symmetrical pockets. Even naked, as he was at the massage house, the professor looks as if he is in a bad disguise.

I remember how he was then, on his back, his gown open on both sides to the floor, his penis sticking from him like a handle. Now, as if he also remembers the same moment, the professor is smiling at me flirtatiously, stopping just short of batting his eyes. He has taken up the volume of erotic poetry again and, tongue caught between teeth, reads a little on one page, a little on another, as he imagines I do late at night while he keeps his vigil on the street below. I feel almost sorry for Professor Mody in Navaz's tight green shirt. He fancies he is offering me his penis—or his *staff of love*, as Yukio would have it—but it is his heart that he surrenders. How much more fully I understand the workings of that four-chambered pump than those cruder hydraulics of love.

28

Desires are already memories.

Now it was my turn to push open the bathroom door without knocking, my turn to stand in that steamy doorway, the proprietary set of my shoulders enabling Lillian only a glimpse—a shirt over the towel rail, the spine's sweet curve to the water, a wet tendril of hair—of the scene I enjoyed fully. Now it was my turn to wait in the dark, above the rustling garden, for a mug of hot brandied milk; my turn to light Navaz's cigarette, the quick flare of the lighter at her lips hollowing her eyes, pegging the shadow of her nose across her face; my turn to wear the same perfume as Navaz, while Lillian moved through the house unscented and alone.

It seems like those should have been the happiest times for me. My mother used an expression like that. She used to say, *the best days of my life*. It always sounded like dirt in her mouth. She would describe some time in her life, long ago, when she was a stranger to all those who knew her now—when she was a girl, say, and on a beach holiday with her mother and father, those grandparents dead before I was born—she would describe some moment when joy was all she knew and then she would say, each word marking out the impassable breach between then and now, *the best days of my life*. My father, my brother and I would hang our heads and turn away as if we were the ones who had snatched her from her idyll, made our miseries hers. She would wrap her arms about her shoulders, holding herself together—or, as it always seemed to me, away from us—with the gratuitous pluckiness of one who has lost an inheritance.

Like the photograph of Navaz and me on either side of the letterbox, my happiest times continue to evade me even when I think I have them fixed. There is always some disquiet, some anxiety, to be remembered. Rewinding my version of events, I find that each happiness is already burrowed through with the mealy trace of the worm. I remember Navaz in the November garden, taking my face in her hands and kissing me on the mouth but still, with everything promised me, I lay afterwards in my bath and felt the water chill around me. The night that Navaz first took me to bed and slept, her thigh heavy across my hips, another weight pressed on me, the thought of Lillian falling through the dark city, her beard perhaps already salted with tears. Even that time during which I slept at Navaz's side while Lillian dreamed alone in my old room, my happiness was precarious and defended every moment against that attack I imagined was imminent. I no longer made luxurious passes down the corridor between Lillian in the kitchen and Navaz in her study but hurried from one to the other in anxious anticipation of what I might find. The sound of their voices from another room, once seeming to speak an intimacy whose generous line included me, now sounded an exclusion, a conspiracy even. There was no longer any pleasure in listening at doorways.

I am left with the souvenirs of that happiness which was never mine: that fickle photograph, Navaz's green shirt, the book by an American poet who spells his name in lower case. I tried spelling my own name like that for a time but it looked smaller than usual, unfinished. Navaz gave me the book late one afternoon in her study. We overlooked the garden where she had kissed me only the week before. I would stand in the same place as it grew dark, not in the hope that Navaz would come out and kiss me again but to remember better the night smells, the last green moment of the basil plants, the warm pressure on my forehead that cooled as Navaz kissed me a second time on the lips. If Navaz saw me put aside my tools at a certain time, stand still as a cat at the edge of the garden, she gave no sign. In the study window, her head remained bent over her work or, wound about with smoke, tilted at the darkening sky. Not quite a gift, she presented me with the book of poetry. That moment when our eyes met and our hands were joined by the width of the book reminded me of other presentations, of prizegivings.

For once Lillian was not in the kitchen. Leaning against Navaz's bookcase, she was our audience. She had the kind of smile that made her seem a party to something. It was that smile, its secret knowledge, that made me self-conscious, made my feet catch on the carpet as I crossed Navaz's study. I was not even sure if the book was a gift or simply another of Navaz's that she was lending me.

'Thanks,' I said and then when that sounded too careless, 'Thank you.' I stroked the book's cover in a way calculated to indicate pleasure but not necessarily possession. Lillian and Navaz were smiling at each other as if they were the ones who had given and received. Lillian put out one hand for the book and, opening it, said, 'We're everything greater than books might mean.' She handed the book back and with its weight again in my hand I understood her to be saying that, whatever paths might be traced by books passing between the three of us, we were bigger than that; bigger, if need be, than Navaz's whole library which climbed from floor to ceiling.

I went and took up my place at the edge of the garden. In the study window I could still see Lillian and Navaz: a line of smoke rose from Navaz's cigarette, seeming to connect her hand with the top of the window frame; Lillian was further back, her head caught against the blurred colour of the books in the study as Navaz's was in *Portrait of the Translator*. They looked like a photograph I would like to have with me now. *We're everything greater than books might mean.* The collection of poetry felt somehow slight and temporary in my hand. It was less convincing out here where the smell of the compost heap hung low to the ground than it had been in the buttery light of the study. I opened the book and saw that Navaz had written a message on the white space beneath the title. *To Helena*—my eye contracted like a shellfish foot when it read my name in Navaz's handwriting—*(we're everything greater/ than books/ might mean) Navaz.*

Lillian had been reading Navaz's message to me. That *we,* which only moments before I had thought Lillian generous enough to extend to me, was suddenly less elastic and passed between Navaz and me like an electric shock. Lillian was still thrown up against the back wall of the study. I could see her there while I waited, book in hand, for the garden to darken and the ghost of Navaz's kiss to sprout on my lips. Navaz had her head back, laughing or exhaling smoke, it was hard to tell from that distance. I remembered the words of another American poet which I tried out loud in the last moments of the day. *It is sad only to be able to mouth other poets; I want someone to mouth me.* It was a night for quotation.

29

I am ready to say goodnight to Professor Mody before his jacket has dried in my bathroom. He seems happy to leave in Navaz's shirt, which he mistakes for mine, his damp jacket rolled into a plastic bag. He fusses over leaving in the shirt.

'I couldn't,' he says, making no move to unbutton. 'I can go bare-chested.' I consider the possibility of his breasts making the distance between my apartment and his. The professor has buttoned the cuffs of the shirt although they only reach half-way down his forearm and the flesh of each arm is squeezed into a ridge by the tight cotton. He stops in my doorway as he likes to do.

'I will return it Monday morning, early.' He strokes himself through the fabric of the shirt as he makes his promise. Once again, I watch from the darkened kitchen window the professor walk through the courtyard. He reaches the bottom of the lane before turning and looking back up at my apartment where I am sure he imagines me to be leafing through a page or two of Yukio before sleep and who knows what dreams. His face has a green cast to it, the street lamp reflected off his borrowed shirt. He blinks at the bottom of the lane for a moment, like the green light at the end of some dock, and is gone.

The weekend passes at the typewriter. I do not know how early the professor intends visiting but on Monday morning I am up at seven, showering before breakfast and making plans for the day. Professor Mody arrives around nine. He has Navaz's shirt, already laundered and wrapped in tissue paper, and an armload of little gifts: two or three more books, a box of chocolates wrapped in foil, a pineapple. He does not seem ill at ease as he usually does. He crosses my threshhold as if it were a finishing tape and busies himself distributing his load about my rooms—the books in my study, the pineapple and chocolates in the kitchen, the shirt in my bedroom. I stand by the front door until he stops moving. Then I say, 'I am going on an expedition. Will you join me?' I have rehearsed this invitation over breakfast, timing the break between sentences. It has just the right tone of invitation and dare. It sounds like something Lillian would say, like a line from an old film.

It was sometimes hard to say whether Lillian was quoting something, a piece of poetry or an advertising slogan, or whether somehow in her mouth everything sounded rounded at the edges, already worn down with use. I hadn't known, for example, that she was quoting the American poet until, outside in the garden, I found her line in his book. In the weeks before Navaz and I left her, as she was making preparations for her 'Same Difference' exhibition, Lillian took to singing around the house, a couple of lines over and over, *My baby thinks she's a train, She don't know the difference between pleasure and pain.* Although there was never any more to the song, I could imagine how the rest might go, a kind of overwritten country blues, my private interior put to music. I followed Lillian about, trawling in the wake of those repeated lines for some expanded meaning, some message. I understood the song to be addressed to me less because I imagined Lillian to be fond of me than because I was sensitive to allegations of stupidity. I never understood how the baby in the song thought she was a train but in the night, with Navaz beside me, a warm smell rising from her sheeted shape, and the scrape of Lillian in a distant room, I would knit and unknit the differences between pleasure and pain, holding them separate one minute, the next unable to tell them apart.

'I am going on an expedition. Will you join me?' Professor Mody slaps his hands on his thighs.

'Certainly,' he says. He does not seem as alarmed as I had imagined: to be honest, he does not seem alarmed at all. He sounds as unconcerned as if I had asked him to join me in a game of tennis. He actually jostles against me in the doorway in his hurry to leave. On the stairs, I see him finger the roll of money in his jacket pocket. Out on the street, I hail a taxi and instruct the driver to take us to the ITDC bus station. The professor sits beside me in the back seat, his hands tucked under his thighs. As we pass the aquarium, he turns to grin at me, his shoulder hunched against his chin, as if the scene at his window, the low sprawl of the building, the queue from the ticket box to the front door, the cloudless sky, are the punch line to some amusing privacy of ours.

The taxi stops outside the station. Professor Mody pays the driver. He stands some distance from the car and hands the note through the driver's window. He cocks his head at me to see whether I am watching.

'Keep the change,' he says, still looking at me. The taxi pulls away but the professor stays bent over the ghost of the car, this time facing the space where the driver's head had been. One of the professor's hands is braced against his leg as he leans towards the open window; the other wags slowly in front of his chest, refusing the money a second time. I think, though I have not thought it before, that he may be a little shorter than me but it is difficult to say when he is standing like this, head at the level of the taxi roof, back bent to follow the curve of its door.

'Keep the change,' he says again. I feel touched, not cheated, that he is replaying that other moment when he was left bookless and bereft, the dust of the taxi's departure settling in the lines of his face. I see how the splay of his hand grips his leg just above the knee and my hand, concealed within my pocket, takes a similar hold of my own thigh.

The station clock says twenty-five past nine. We are early. The bus is already standing at its bay but the driver is nowhere about. Rather than wait aimlessly with the professor at my side or even take up seats on the empty bus, I walk the few blocks down to the sea front. It is a little cooler down here than it was in the forecourt of the bus station. I sit on the stone wall, my back to the stench coming off the water. The professor tries to hop up beside me; another man approaches, carrying a wicker basket full of laundry. He has bare feet and a cloth wound about his head.

'Madam,' he says. 'Sir.' He does not turn his head to where the professor has finally managed to mount the wall, one leg thrown across its width as if he were riding a horse, facing the wrong way, across to Nariman Point. The man is smiling and smiling. He looks as if he could stop at any moment.

'You are American,' he tells me. He begins to remove the towel from the top of his laundry basket. Something stirs in the darkness. I move my feet further up the wall. I think of snakes, of muscular contractions beneath cold, dry skin. The professor is trying to turn around. He looks over his shoulder at where the basket lies open on the pavement.

'Madam only needs to look,' says the man. And I am looking. My legs rising to the top of the wall, my body turned towards the professor, I fix my eyes on whatever is shifting, not quite visible, at the bottom of the basket.

Before I see the snake, the man removes a flute from the front of his shirt. He squats down, plays a few notes, a few more; kicks at the basket with his foot. A snake uncoils from the shadows, sways for a moment, hood flared. I think there is the pattern of a person's face in the scales on the back of its head, two eyes, a nose, a mouth even. My own face seems suddenly unable to move, its features as fixed as patterns picked out in coloured scales. Another snake has unwound itself from the basket. It is interested less in the flute playing and the swaying back and forth of the first snake than lying in the sun on the pavement. Still playing, the snake-charmer gives this snake a stir with the end of his flute. It is seeing the snake's skin pucker where it is touched by the end of the flute that decides me.

'Stop him,' I say to Professor Mody. The professor is himself swaying from side to side but looking down the road to where a traffic pointsman is arguing with a motorist. He looks at me for a moment, then slipping off the wall, almost stands on the snake which is sunning itself on the warm asphalt.

'Stop,' he says to the snake-charmer. The professor produces several coins from his pocket and hands them to the man whose silent flute still hangs from his lips. He adds something in another language and the snake-charmer wags his head from side to side in agreement, looking up to where I sit on the wall, legs still drawn beneath me. He picks the snake up from the pavement as casually as if this were a laundry basket after all and the snake some sock left lying where it fell the night before. He shakes the first snake down, throws the other on top and replaces the piece of towelling. The professor switches to English.

'Get a move on, young fellow,' he says, his excitement skewing his idiom. 'I'll have no pranks before the lady.' The snake-charmer is packed up now. He jangles the coins in thanks once, twice, on his open palm. Basket held against his chest, he moves off, the twin rudders of his shoulder blades cutting a course for a group of tourists further along the walk.

'Move along if you don't want a drubbing,' calls the professor at his back.

Back at the station, the bus has its engine running. Professor Mody and I line up at the ticket office.

'Bombay suburbs,' I say to the clerk who turns out to be also the bus driver. I turn to the professor but he is not to be caught out. He has his money roll in his hand already, pays for the tickets and passes them over to me without demur.

'Boarding in five minutes,' says the clerk. The professor is pleased with himself. He walks in little bouncy steps, on the balls of his feet.

'Bombay suburbs,' he says to me. And then, reading off the side of the bus, 'Vihar Lake. Aarey Milk Colony. Krishnagiri Upavan National Park.'

'Have you visited these places before?' I ask.

'Not with you,' the professor says gallantly, standing aside at the bus door, one hand raised to assist me.

We settle ourselves in a double seat towards the back of the bus. The professor wants to talk. He explains the interchange he had with the snake-charmer in which he claims the man wanted to show me how safe his snakes were by demonstrating how they are milked of their venom. This subject disturbs me so, before the bus has even started I pretend to fall asleep. The last thing I see before my eyelids close is the professor's hand, raised like a shadow puppet of a snake, making exploratory lunging motions at the bare skin of his other arm.

30

Once Navaz and I started sleeping together, the house began to withhold itself from me a little. Secrets flourished everywhere: they grew green and sturdy as my tomato plants, in glances I imagined Navaz and Lillian exchanged behind my back, in the spaces between words at the breakfast table. I say *sleeping together* but it's just a turn of phrase, I don't remember a great deal of that. When I remember Navaz's bed, I am always awake. I am pressing my face against the crook of Navaz's neck, against the mattress, or labouring silently over her, not allowing Lillian to overhear the slightest evidence of my thrall. Or else I am lying beside Navaz, who sleeps with one leg thrown across my hips, listening for the sounds of the house running down for the night, for Lillian's movement in the room opposite.

That anxiety I once had about leaving the house returned to me. When I was living at my aunt's house, I put off going home for the night in part for fear of what Lillian and Navaz might say of me in my absence. When I shifted in with them, into that lamp-lit room and that single bed laid as carefully as a trap, I felt as though I never had to leave. There was no sense of exclusion. I moved from Lillian to Navaz and back again not to see what they transacted between them but as if I were the thing that held them together. Now when I got up and dressed for my downtown job, it was with a sense that the house had another life, a life predicated on my being elsewhere. If Lillian were not up by the time I left or if Navaz stayed in bed, watching me dress but not joining me for breakfast, then I walked to work knowing how other clothes would now be being removed, how Lillian would be crying out, back arched against Navaz's hand as mine had been only the night before. Then all that sweetness would rewrite itself as already in the past tense: I would return home this evening to find myself demoted to the single bed, my loss of wilder possibilities brought home to me most literally by its narrow reach.

Nor was it any comfort to think of the two of them engaged less strenuously, sitting at the kitchen table over a pot of tea or, in the afternoon, with half a bottle of wine at their elbows, talking to each other in that way I could never manage. I mean that 'manage' to indicate inability not intolerance; I appreciated it but as my parents' friends claim to 'appreciate' music or theatre, all pleasure in such arts underwritten by their remoteness from its production. They would talk about me, of course—Navaz would placate Lillian with small betrayals, tell her my family nickname or how I always took my socks off last—or worse, my name would not come up. Other matters would occupy them, my absence from the house licensing them not to speak unguardedly of me but to ignore me altogether. Except for Lillian's daily appearance in my queue at the bank, I had no idea of their routines. I would always ask Navaz when I came in how much of Nishimura's novel she had translated, disguising my project of ascertaining how much time she had spent in legitimate pursuits as a more benign interest in her day.

Lillian had started working on her 'Same Difference' exhibition. Usually by the time I came to the kitchen for breakfast she was already there, matching samples of cloth to paint charts, sketching cartoons of her planned dozen photographs. There was always a slight awkwardness between us, less because I had just come from Navaz's bed than because she would be dressed in my clothes and eating what was recognisably my breakfast, grapefruit and cereal. I was not quite sure what was meant by 'same difference' and was surprised enough to ask the first time I heard it mentioned. It was one afternoon when I had worked through my lunch hour and come home earlier than usual. I had already imagined just how it would be: the back of the house open on to the afternoon garden, the radio playing unattended in the kitchen, and the bedroom door ajar as in a horror movie. Still, imagining all this, I expected the house to be as it always was, Lillian working on some papier mâché prop in the kitchen, Navaz smoking at her desk.

Instead, it was the front door that was open. In the living room, Navaz was lying naked on the couch. I did not recognise the couch immediately because it was pulled away from the wall and made up with one of the white sheets from our bed. Navaz was up on one elbow, the pile of cushions at her back supporting her in an almost sitting position. She had a pink hibiscus tucked behind her left ear and a black shoelace tied in a bow around her neck. When she saw me in the doorway, she swung her legs over the edge of the couch, started to sit up. Lillian stood up from where she had been crouching out of sight behind the couch. She was draped in the other bedsheet and had a white handerkerchief wound tight as a skullcap around her head.

'O, it's you,' Lillian says, seeing me over Navaz's naked shoulder. She seems almost to have expected me. 'We'll break for five minutes.' Navaz removes the hibiscus, places it with care on one of the cushions and walks from the room. She seems in no hurry to get dressed.

'What are you doing?' I am pleased to hear my voice come out with a measured amount of curiosity and disinterest.

'We're starting to shoot the "Same Difference" exhibition,' says Lillian, still fussing with a basket of flowers. That 'we' is not lost on me.

'"Same Difference"?' I try to disguise my question as a criticism or, at least, a sneer but Lillian recognises it for the inquiry it is. She puts aside her basket for a moment and starts in on an explanation which will, I am sure, make it into the exhibition catalogue.

'As a term, "same difference" describes the double bind of female representation in a representational system which is unable to register difference from itself. "Same difference", which a dictionary of colloquial usage will tell you is no difference at all, articulates the difficulty of placing female sexuality in relation to a phallocentric system of representation which structures itself around notions of visibility.' My bank uniform suddenly seems more absurd in this room than Lillian's double sheet or the black shoelace which is still the only thing that Navaz has on when she returns. I hand her a dressing gown, pretending that I thought she had been looking for it.

Navaz takes up her position again on the couch with the professional boredom of the nude model. She slots the hibiscus behind her right ear.

'Other ear,' says Lillian, smearing some word at the end of her sentence which might have been 'love' or 'hon'. Lillian is putting me in my place with her *phallocentric* and *articulates*. You might be sleeping in her bed at the moment, she is telling me, but you couldn't call her by anything but her name. I have a bad-tempered urge to fix myself a drink and watch some television with my feet up.

'Stand behind the camera,' Lillian says to me and to Navaz, 'Left leg over right at the knee.' Lillian starfishes Navaz's hand over her pubic area, stands back a few paces studying her with her head on one side.

'Its perfect,' she says. 'Now hold it.' I hate Lillian for making me see Navaz's body like this, as unmoving yet biddable, as having *a pubic area*. I do not really hate her but nevertheless between her instruction and her arrangement of Navaz's hand comes the moment when I begin to make my plan.

Lillian leaves the room. Navaz's stare goes out blankly without hitting its mark. I bend to the camera, seeing if I can catch her eye through its intervention but her gaze is pitched just lower again. Lillian returns with the neighbour's black kitten in a wire cage.

'Close the door,' she says to me, still bent over the camera. It is not clear how she might have conducted her operation if I had not returned home earlier than expected. The kitten is very agreeable. It curls up on the end of the couch, closes its little pink and white mouth, its green eyes, and disappears in blackness. Lillian prods it; she stands it up; she holds it under its belly, bending its back into a horseshoe shape.

'He has to arch his back,' she says with a note of complaint, as if the cruelty were all the kitten's. 'How can I frighten him without making him jump off the bed? Don't move your head or you'll lose the flower. Maybe he'd be frightened of his reflection. Bring me a mirror.' All the time, she is stretching the kitten's tail over his back, poking his belly with her finger, and he is purring and rubbing his face against the back of her hand. Now he sits down, puts one back leg over his shoulder and begins licking under his tail.

'Come back, come back,' calls Lillian, catching up the basket of flowers and standing behind the couch, level with Navaz's feet.

'It's perfect. Take the picture.' She tilts the basket at the camera as if she were a waiter offering a bottle of wine for inspection, looks sidelong at Navaz so only the whites of her eyes show. I push one likely button, then another. There is a flash of light. The shadow of Navaz's hibiscus is thrown up on the back wall. Later it turns out that I have rearticulated Édouard Manet's *Olympia*.

31

The bus seems to have little suspension over its rear wheels. Professor Mody and I are thrown about, bounced down and up to a perverse rhythm as if the warm vinyl seat were the broad back of some little pony. I can no longer pretend to be sleeping. Across the aisle a man and a woman are sitting with their legs crossed on the seat. They are unpacking a meal from a basket on the seat between them, scraping up some near soupy mix with pieces of soft, round bread. The woman sees me watching her across the aisle. She exaggerates her bouncing movements, waggling her head and smiling at me. She tilts her head back and lowers the bread parcels into her mouth from a little height.

From the window, I see the sign for the Aarey Milk Colony. I have not quite known what to expect: its name makes me think of something reclusive and clinical like a sanatorium. There are two buses already pulled up at the gates and, when we stop alongside, a brass band begins a wheezy tune. In the gateway, a group of schoolchildren are assembled. Their hands are behind their backs, they are arranged according to height, but already they have started to wilt in the heat like seedlings watered in the morning. Our busdriver stands in the aisle with his arms raised. He waits for our attention.

'Ladies and gentlemen,' he says, over what sounds like the band's last breath. 'Today one million buses have arrived at the milk colony. Please join in the celebration.'

I do not believe in the million buses for the busdriver makes his announcement routinely and there is no banner or placard to explain the band and the waiting schoolchildren. I think every busload is met with the same tired aplomb. Our busdriver waits until we all get down, then he herds us into a group and, packed between the other two tour groups, we face the children across a bright stretch of bleached ground.

The band members are elderly and, close up, there are not really enough of them for a band. One of then steps forward, trumpet in hand, and announces that among our group is the millionth visitor to the milk colony. He raises his instrument to his lips and behind him, although not quite with him, his ragged band plays. The children begin to sing some impossible song which seems in danger of tearing away from the tune altogether. They execute a dance in small, parade-ground marching steps and produce from behind their backs wooden batons which they pass from hand to hand. The sound of their feet scraping in the dust is easily heard over the band. Professor Mody is standing beside me, the pressure of the crowd allowing him this closeness. He tries to direct my attention to something which is amusing him but our busdriver stops him with a cautioning eyebrow. At the end of their item, the children break ranks and run towards us, presenting each of us with one of their batons. We clap. It feels better to be doing something in this heat. I lean towards the child who runs to me with his baton, think I hear him say, 'Happy New Year' as he lets go of his end and returns to his friends. My baton has red writing painted on its side: *Aarey Milk—Creamy! Dreamy!*

We are allowed to file through the gates at last. The children stand to one side as we pass. At first I think they are singing again, a slow song, but then I realise that they are counting, a number chanted every time one of us moves through the gate. I don't recognise the numbers, don't know what they are up to yet, but suddenly I see how it will all work out. The professor will be the millionth visitor. Even now, unknowing, he moves before me in line, the shape of his head just visible through his thinning hair, the back of his neck creased in soft folds. The children's voices grow more shrill as the professor passes under the gate, as I pass after him, and the bandmaster steps from the shade of the gate and drapes a garland over the shoulders of the man in the line behind me. The trumpets sound and the garlanded man is led to the front of the group that we might all see what it is to be the millionth visitor. There is, of course, nothing to be done. I eat lunch at the Aarey Garden Restaurant and take in the view from the top of the hill with the professor at my side, his ordinary shoulders bowed down with the weight of nothing more than the epaulettes on his safari-suit jacket.

The road to the national park looks like the turn-off to a city tip; stunted shrubs, the very dust rising from the bus tyres smells of excrement. I remember how tiring it is to be moving oneself around like this. The mistake is to think of travelling as a way of making oneself more substantial when all the time the increase is in the other direction; one becomes less and less, leaving a little behind at each stop. There are more caves to see, Buddhist ones with carvings and, Professor Mody tells me, bats flying about, squeaking in the dark. I seem to have lost my interest in caves but I get down with the others, and while they enter the third cave, the Great Chaitya, I stand in the shade and watch some monkeys rolling in the dust, throwing themselves up and down trees. The professor is unsure what to do. At first he follows the group into the cave but when he sees that I am not following he veers away to one side as if he never intended going in. Now he stands a little distance from me, pretending to find some charm in a small and scraggy bush growing from a rock. Over its dusty leaves, he glances at me now and then. Soon our party herds through the cave entrance and towards the bus. The fool who won the garland at the milk colony is still wearing it. He poses for one final photograph outside the cave, arranging the flowers across his chest as if they had been awarded to him again.

Back in the bus, I ignore the professor. We are driven a short way before stopping in a small compound.

'Gentlemen,' says the busdriver, forgetting the 'ladies' in his hurry to make his announcement. 'The lion safari park. Please dismount and wait for the safari bus.'

I make the professor ask why we have to change buses: there was no mention of this previously.

'Please,' says Professor Mody from our seat towards the back of the bus. 'Why are we to change buses? There was no mention made of this in your publicity.' He uses my words almost exactly. The people who have been collecting their belongings and filing down the aisle stop and look from the professor to the busdriver.

'This is only an ordinary bus,' says the busdriver. 'For road travel.

But in the safari park you will be carried safely inside a safari bus. Much stronger, you see.' Everyone starts to move again. As we pass the busdriver, he takes Professor Mody by the arm and says, 'Stainless steel reinforced. Window bars.'

We wait for the safari bus to arrive. Ahead of us there are sixteen-foot wire fences enclosing the park. There is a gate, wound through with barbed wire and secured with a fist-sized padlock, where the road meets the fence and, forty feet into the park, a second gate. The Bombay suburbs bus drives away, perhaps for refuelling or to keep cool in the shade somewhere. The professor takes my arm as the busdriver took his and says, 'Window bars. Stainless steel reinforced.' He keeps a grip on my arm as he looks into the safari park, down the road and across the two gates, where there is some movement, something brown and low to the ground, travelling towards the fenceline. Some of the others have noticed something or are trying to see what has caught Professor Mody's attention. A few of those with cameras move towards the gate, reassure themselves with its height before putting their eyes to the viewfinder and pointing their lens down the track. Whatever it is must be following the line of the road itself. The sun catches on something behind the last straggle of bushes. The professor's hand tightens on my arm as three men emerge into the open, carrying bales of greenery on their heads or shoulders, their legs pale with dust from the knees down.

They do not seem to realise that they are in a safari park; they chat to each other or rather they talk to each other's backs, unable to turn their heads under the load that buckles their knees. The garlanded man squeezes off a few exposures but it is only to save face. He does not have a telephoto lens and at this distance, through the wire of the two gates, the men are almost lost in the scenery, their heads swathed in green, their legs the same colour as the road. They approach the second gate and, without putting down their bundles, they push it open and pass through. The last man, but I see now they are only boys, kicks the gate shut behind him. Professor Mody lets go of my hand as the boys walk towards us. As if in a film, the boys' outlines blur as I focus twenty feet in front of them, on the brass weight of the padlock, which I haven't imagined, securing the gate to the fence. At the gate, the boys throw down their bushels. One peels back a section of fence, as casually as if he were holding open a door, another passes through the gap and, one pushing, one pulling, they soon have all the bamboo leaves, if that is what they are, on our side of the fence. They help each other hoist their burdens to head height once more and move down the road a little before breaking off and making through the waist-high scrub on some imagined path.

32

Navaz and I made one last trip out of the city before she left me. I didn't know then that she was about to leave me so our trip was only 'last' in retrospect. I preferred it that way. I slept at night without the guilty thought that I should be watching her sleep beside me, memorising the weight of her leg across me, the rise and fall of the sheet across her back. I visited the various churches and took no commemorative pictures: Navaz outside Se Cathedral, Navaz in front of the mural depicting St Francis Xavier's death on Sancian Island, Navaz at the entrance to the Basilica of Bom Jesus. As was our habit, I had not consulted Navaz about the trip but bought the tickets myself after seeing from the airline timetable that we could make the round trip within three days. We flew from the city late Tuesday afternoon and had return tickets for Friday morning.

At the airport, our flight had been delayed for three hours. The airline directed us to a hotel across the road for what they called a 'lunch' although if the hour were any consideration it was more like a children's tea. Navaz excuses herself from the table and returns yellow and waxy as cheese rind. She pushes her plate away and takes small sips of water, only wetting her lips really, as if she fears poisoning.

'You're not well.' It sounds like an accusation. Already I see how we will have to cancel our tickets; how Navaz's family will take over, perhaps even accommodating her in their house until she is well.

'It's just the delay,' Navaz says, although she has not proved so delicate before. I am ashamed of myself.

'We will cancel our tickets or postpone them until later in the week,' I say.

'Not necessary.' Navaz has sweat at her hairline. She continues to take birdlike dips into her glass of water.

'Let me at least ring your aunt and see what she has to say.' There is no doubt what the aunt would say. A car would be dispatched to the airport before I had even hung up the telephone.

'No. Can you imagine?' She creases her eyes at me across the table. 'Perhaps it was something I ate. I feel better now.'

And she looks better, better than she did. As you are my witness, she wanted to go.

I do not ask Navaz again how she is feeling but I watch her for signs of unease. She eats nothing during the flight and when the taxi drops us at our hotel, although she makes some show of taking in the view from our balcony, she soon is lying on the bed, not quite sleeping, her breath coming fast through dry lips. There is nothing to do in our room. I stand on the balcony and watch the river. Behind me, I imagine I can hear Navaz working her breath in and out. I pull a cover over her and keep watch. When I lift her hair off her forehead with the back of my hand, her skin feels hot and dry. She says something but won't repeat it when I bend my ear to her mouth. Her lips are coated with something white and stick to her teeth in places.

In the morning, she is better. With a warm washcloth, I clean the corners of her eyes, her lips, damp her hair back from her face. She gets up and cleans her teeth, stands on our balcony in her dressing gown, her mouth foaming, toothbrush in hand. I run a shower for her and watch while she washes her hair. Even though she is recovered, I can't take my eyes from her. From under the water, and not knowing how close I am, Navaz calls, 'I'm starving.' We will go out for breakfast, some pancakes and fruit at a riverside restaurant.

'What did you have for dinner last night?' There had been no dinner. I suppose I could have left Navaz for half an hour and eaten in the hotel dining room but something kept me here. It didn't feel like deprivation. I hung over Navaz, sponging her down, changing her T-shirt when she soaked it through. For an hour or so, when she was quieter, I let her hold my index finger, making a fist around it as babies will do. Yet whatever feeling that was that brought me close to tears, happiness stretching like a ligament in my chest, could hardly be called maternal. It had a rough cast to it, a raw edge. It wasn't that I put aside thoughts of myself and tended to Navaz. All the time I was bending over her sleeptalking or leaving her naked longer than necessary while I helped her into a fresh shirt, while my hand was at her forehead in a showy checking of her temperature or at her wrist idly feeling her blood bump against my fingers, I was not thinking of her as my charge, my child, but of the pleasing contrast of my hand on her head, of the hot passage between her mouth and my ear. There are only a couple of hours of last night that I cannot account for but I don't need sleep. This morning, watching Navaz in the shower, the water falling across her upturned face and into her mouth, I feel bigger than myself. I am surprised to see myself looking so ordinary in the misted mirror: I should be charged with radiance, like those Christmas figures with a lightbulb inside.

We walk down the block for breakfast, keeping the river on our right. It is as if my imagination has gone before us, arranging the world as I would have it, for here is a restaurant with a view to the river and pancakes and fruit on the menu. I see that Navaz is not yet relaxed about food. As if it were a small bony fish, she eats her pancake in small forkfuls with much chewing. She reads the guidebook I have brought with us, holding it open on the table with her spare hand.

'A half day at the churches,' she says, 'and on to the beach this afternoon.' This was my original plan. There is not enough to do in town to keep us occupied for even three days but now, with Navaz unwell, I think it would be better to stay here in a hotel, near the hospital and only two hours flight from the city.

'But it's only a few hours on the bus,' says Navaz. 'I could just lie about on a shaded beach.' Who could deny her anything? Her bones seem closer to the surface of her face this morning. Her cheekbone rests in her hand as if it were the rim of a cup. I wonder whether she really wants to go up the coast or whether she only offers for fear of denying me pleasure. I would as easily stay here with her, would as easily have two more nights like the last one, but there is no way of saying this that does not sound like gallantry.

We take the bus to Margao that afternoon. Navaz sleeps with her cheek against the glass. Every time the bus ventures on to a rickety bridge, disregarding the signposted warning *Caution: weak bridge ahead*, I hold her sleeping hand, wonder what last words I might manage, shaking her awake as the cab fills up with brackish water. The bus stops every kilometre or so, picking up people from the side of the road, dropping others. There do not seem to be any bus stops, just these clumps of travellers measuring out the road between the town and the beach. The conductor moves down the crowded aisle, collecting fares. He remembers each face, never asks twice for the same fare, walks across the back of the seats when the crush is too thick to move through. Navaz twitches in her sleep. Who knows what dreams are substituting themselves for this ride? Coconut palms, yellow and purple bougainvillea, little white churches are framed in the bus window like postcards from my aunt but who knows what images are playing themselves out behind Navaz's retina? I barely take my eyes from her. It is as if her health is a performance which depends on my vigilance as spectator. I note a vein jump in her eyelid, the way her palm turns in her lap like a fish. I am taken up with the simple narrative of her inhalations and exhalations.

At Margao, we hire a taxi for the last leg of our journey. Colva looks like a stage set when we pull into the late afternoon square. Everything faces inwards like false fronting and the sea in the background looks touched up, filmed through a blue gel. Our accommodation—or *chalet*, in the words of the advertisement—is five minutes away along the beach. It has a living room and bathroom downstairs and a bedroom upstairs. As is common with stairs, there is an urge to climb them immediately, to stand in the tallest possible place, to assert ourselves over an unknown space. At the bedroom window, the sloped ceiling just clears our heads. We turn back the covers, the cool promise of white sheets; we lie together, clothed, not quite touching, testing the pillows for comfort. If there were no trees lining the shore road, we could see the water from our bed.

33

The safari bus arrives, its horn seeming to sound over a distance like a ship's siren. It stops in front of the park gates and much is made of the fact that the driver's assistant must unlock the door from the inside before we are able to board. He jangles a ring of keys at us through the glass. Over the noisy shudder of the engine's idle, it is a dumbshow but we appreciate the gesture even while we are amused by its excess. We file on board, the professor and I making sure to get seats closer to the front this time. As a group, we seem better when we are moving, when we are run together and expected to complete some simple chore. With time on our hands, we remember we are strangers, some centrifugal force has us falling away from our untraversable core. Out in the open, unsupervised, our attention directed at nothing in particular, we can barely glance at each other, our faces raw against the wide stretch of the landscape. Back in the tight space of a bus, we are reassured of each other's proximity; we see more readily what we have in common.

The driver puts the bus in gear and passes through the first gate, now unlocked and held open by the tour guide. The guide rides on the outside of the bus, standing on the bottom step and holding the rail, until we reach the second gate which he opens. He reboards the bus and locks the door behind him, letting us see that he double-checks the padlock, throws his slight weight once, twice, against the door panelling. He shakes the keys at us again before sliding them into his pocket: this time we hear their clatter and scrape. Pulling on a peaked cap, he straddles the aisle and begins to deliver his commentary. The guide holds on to a seat with each hand but still he is thrown from side to side and his voice reaches us in clumps, the rattle of the bus engine seeming to have caught in his throat.

'. . . your security is uppermost . . . please to enjoy the oldest . . . today our driver . . .' Here the guide's voice is lost completely as he turns away from us, swivelling his head at the driver who seems somehow to recognise his cue, lifts one arm from the bucking steering wheel and waves, smiles at us in the juddering square of the rear vision mirror.

Inside the game park seems much like outside; the same scrubby bush, dust, some kind of buffalo grass in patches and no sign of anything that might be called game. Nor do we seem to be taking the slow, circuitous patrol that I had imagined, the guide drawing our attention to the spoor of elephant and antelope, the flattened patches of grass at the edge of the lake which mark the passing of the water buffalo, before directing the driver behind a grass hide and commenting on the wildlife which unspools like a nature documentary through the insect-streaked glass of the windscreen. Instead, the bus is being driven at speed along the road which strikes unengagingly into the distance, scoring the plain into identical halves. A mile or two down the track, the guide resumes his patter.

'The male of the species . . . according to age and strength . . . aren't they the lucky ones?'

I glance at Professor Mody whose face is arranged without fault, attentive but not quite engaged. And there is something else about him that I can't put my finger on, that I will describe to him later as his having 'the mark of the chosen about him'. I saw it first as we filed through the gate at the milk colony; I see it again now in the greasy spray of light that comes through the dirty window beside the professor.

The guide is pointing out the windows on the right hand side of the bus.

'Yesterday a group of seven . . . regular sightings last week.' It seems that he is talking about lions, an animal I had forgotten to include in my imagined populating of the park. First two or three, and then everyone, sitting on the left-hand side of the bus crams into the aisle, leaning over those of us already sitting on this side, to stare at the place where lions were sighted yesterday. The site seems unexceptional, so unexceptional I was not even sure if I had the right spot. By the time most of them are on their feet, that particular patch of grassy dust is fifty metres behind us and sliding fast to the horizon. Now the guide taps the driver's shoulder, the bus crashes down through its gears, slows to walking pace.

'Our first lion, ladies and gentlemen,' says the guide, forgetting, for the first time, to point. We crane in every direction to no effect. Now that there is no difficulty in hearing his every word, the perverse guide begins to ration himself.

And here is the first lion, almost under the wheels of the bus, sunning itself on the road and unwilling to move aside even under the horn's louring persuasion. The crush of people in the aisle grows more dense as if reducing the distance between oneself and the lion outdoes the simple pleasure of seeing it. The guide himself has his face smeared against the glass—I can see the peak of his khaki cap pushed back against the window—and he explains to those who will listen that this is 'Mr Lion', that the rest of his family must be nearby. Few pay him any attention; in delivering the lion to them he has served his purpose. They bang on the glass, tap against it with the bodies of their cameras and make the roaring noises they hope to hear from the lion. The lion continues to throw its coat in the sun; it looks as if it has not moved, let alone roared, today. Its body seems too small for its head; like a glove puppet, it lies heavily in the dust, eyes closed. Every now and then its tail switches, its body—fur nubbed and worn down in patches like a favourite teddy bear—rises and falls with its panting breath. The busdriver, after several more useless blasts on the horn, runs off the road, driving around the lion with one set of wheels in the ditch. I think for a moment that the bus may tip on its side and in that imagined disaster—will we be able to unlock the door or will it come to rest against the ground, the barred windows mocking our chances of escape?—the lion does not even figure as an anxiety.

Once the bus is level again, both sets of wheels back on the road, and the lion slowly falling away into the middle distance behind us, everyone resumes their seats.

'Coming up on your left,' says the guide, 'is Mr Lion's family.' This time everyone sitting on our side of the bus stands and crowds into the aisle determined to see the view of those who had so recently poached theirs. There is a restrained struggle: those standing lean as far forward as they can while keeping their faces fixed on the yellow and brown landscape that slides past the windows; those sitting turn in their seats, offering their stiff shoulders and the backs of their heads to the aisle. The professor and I are the only ones left sitting on this side of the bus. There is no point even turning our heads; we will see nothing through the crush of backs and buttocks turned against us.

'Two lionesses. The darker animal is the young male's mother.' The guide is still standing in the aisle and his voice carries easily to us across the backs of those tapping against the glass and roaring low in their throats.

'The young fellow is about two years old.' The bus has not quite stopped and, judging by the knot of people that moves towards the back of the coach, the group of lions drifts by as if in a slipstream.

'Perhaps you do not find the lions so interesting?' The guide has noticed our defection and insults us with that elaborate courtesy which is always unanswerable. The roaring from the back of the bus stops, whether because the lions have passed from view or because we are suddenly more intriguing is not clear.

'Not at all,' says the professor, inclining his head towards the guide with faked respect. 'We were very interested in Mr Lion. Was he sleeping, do you think, or was he dead?'

There is a flurry from those still standing behind us: I hear the word 'dead' repeated in varying tones and in a scornful voice I credit to the garlanded man, 'His ribs are moving.'

'Dead?' The guide moves towards us down the aisle. 'Dead? Would you think my lions were dead if you were to step down from the safety of my bus?' He almost forgets to pretend politeness; he extends the possessive pronoun to include both the bus and the lions. The rest of the tour party crowd to the side of our double seat and look at the professor with a new interest. I also have a new interest in the professor. He seems to be smirking, although his lips do not curl. It is an entirely internal smirk, evident only in the way he hunches his usually pinned-back shoulders, as if he were restraining himself from laughing at some joke we would not understand, perhaps even some joke at our expense. The safari park rolls yellow and brown, unseen, past his bowed shoulder.

'Would you like to step down from the safety of our bus?' Now the bus belongs to everyone except the professor who turns to me and smiles like a rubberband.

I have a feeling that I have seen all this before. I am on the verge of knowing what is to happen next but I can't think what that is exactly until each subsequent action reminds me and I say to myself not, 'So that's how it all turns out' but, 'Yes, that's it, that's it.' *Déja-vu*, we say in French, as if we haven't the words for it; as if what we have seen before happened in another country, another language. The professor lifts his shoulders in a scaled-down shrug and I remember this too, this little sketch of diffidence, as if once before it happened in exactly this way. But there's something else I can't quite recall, like a movement seen out of the corner of my eye. The professor purses his lips in a drawstring moue and I instantly recognise that pout as what I have been waiting for. He stands. It is just as it should be. Does he speak now? Am I to do something? He arranges his safari jacket fastidiously, brushing twice, three times, at an invisible strand of cotton before he is satisfied. He remembers it all more clearly than I do and he plays it out without a flaw. I sit entranced, like the woman from Leeds in the *Guinness Book of Records* who saw *The Sound of Music* eighty-six times. My pleasure is fashioned after complacency. The professor's voice is perfectly cadenced, rising and falling as it should.

'Unlock the door and I should be happy to step out for a few minutes,' says Professor Mody. The tour party falls back from the professor as if he were the lion; there is the clinking of metal on metal as the guide unlocks, then throws open, the door. One hand blocking the fall of light to his face, the professor hesitates as he likes to do in doorways, looks back at me as if at his accomplice. It is all coming out like a slow hand of patience.

34

When Lillian took to dressing in my clothes and eating my breakfast, she also began to neglect some of those chores in which she had once seemed to take a pleasure. Perhaps it was simply that she was taken up with the demands of preparing her new exhibition, but if she were to be found in the kitchen these evenings, she was no longer reducing a beer and fig sauce for a rabbit casserole or forcing open shellfish with an oyster knife. More likely, she was bent over a magnifying glass, studying sheets of negatives on her light table or drying gold-painted baubles in front of a bar heater. The kitchen no longer felt like the heart, the guts of the house. Sometimes Navaz or I would hang in the doorway as one stands a moment outside the house of a former lover or across the street from a restaurant where the two of you used to dine. Then, with the fumes of paint or glue in our noses, we would remember better days when the kitchen shone like a yellow eye, when on our second bottle of sauvignon blanc, Lillian would have us spooning the meat from blue swimmer crabs while she strained the rest of the soup through a muslin bag.

Lillian is not saying much these days. When she sees either Navaz or me standing in the kitchen doorway, she bends her head over her work without saying a word. She thinks she is demonstrating her speechlessness but I can read these little vignettes of hers as clearly as if they had subtitles tracking across the bottom. Last night I put my head around the doorjamb to see Navaz scraping some toast out from under the griller. The curve of Lillian's shoulder, the way her head hung over the table like a hammer, said quite distinctly, *without me, you're nothing*. I saw at once how we were nothing without her. This alarms me because the plan I am now formulating operates without Lillian; indeed it is a plan which will be realised when we disengage ourselves from her. Lillian imagines she has the luxury of a long campaign. She can't see how she could lose. She doesn't know that I speak with Navaz in a low voice late at night when sleep is a heartbeat away and everything seems possible.

The kitchen has become a sad place but seeing Navaz toasting bread at the griller decides me. Navaz is not a person who looks good cooking. I hope you understand me when I say this. She looks good with a glass of wine, a cigarette sending up a signal from a nearby ashtray. With a plate of food in front of her, she is elegant. She knows the names of things: *carpe à l'oseille, galantine, rouille*. But when she herself has to cook, when she puts on Lillian's apron, food seems suddenly crude. She does not attempt anything fancy but even her simple assembling of cheese, eggs and milk for a rarebit reminds me that food is for pleasure second, for survival first; that food is most literally something which keeps us from death. Something about the careful way Navaz handles food deprives it of its innocence. Under her hand, eggs are no longer symbols of wholesomeness and vitality, milk is no longer shorthand for purity. Under her hand, food seems to have a history. It points to its origin and destination, drawing a connection between the blood-specked and feathered backsides of chickens, the complacent udders of the cow and—more than our faces, over the table, chewing and swallowing—that other mouth, never mentioned at the dining table, which spits food from our bodies in private. I take the knife from Navaz's hand—it feels like disarming someone—and make rarebit for the three of us.

The next day I come home with a plastic bag of groceries and something more cunning in the side pouch of my briefcase. Once again the couch is pulled away from the living room wall and made up with the white sheet from the double bed. This time both Navaz and Lillian are naked. I recognise a scene I have yet to see. Navaz is lying on her back, one hip turned under her so her buttocks face the door. Lillian rests her head on Navaz's shoulder, her leg under Navaz's thigh while, one hand at the calf, she supports Navaz's other leg across her hip. Both are feigning sleep: Navaz flushed at the cheeks, Lillian not quite frowning as if some dream were worrying at her. On the sheet at the bottom of the bed, between their tangle of feet, are two of my earrings and the pearled hair spike Lillian wears when she dresses as Mrs Simpson. A vase of my sweetpeas stands behind the bed on the television table which has been done up with papier mâché curlicues. The camera is set on automatic and every few seconds its flash goes off, flattening the room with its wash of white light.

I do not even put my bag of groceries down. I tiptoe towards the kitchen as if Lillian and Navaz really were sleeping in the front room. From Lillian's sketches, I know already that this is Gustave Courbet's *Sleep*, or as I prefer, favouring its alternative title, *Idleness and Luxury*. Tonight we will eat in the kitchen again. Not being able to match Lillian's style, I plan to make a virtue out of simplicity: a leg of lamb with garlic and rosemary under the skin, roast vegetables and gravy. The sound of the flash going off at the end of the corridor sounds like the regular fizz of a neon sign. I remember the sound of the neon sign outside the Tonks Avenue tattoo parlour *Clean needles American designs*. I remember again a scene I have yet to see.

Navaz will be just as she is now in the front room, eyes closed yet contracting under the orange flare of the flashlight seen through the thin skin of her eyelids. Outside will be the sounds of the night courtyard, the cough of the watchman, the houseboy's bad dream. Navaz will be just as she is now, her head back against the pillow, the flush of her fever still in her cheeks. And I will have taken Lillian's place, Navaz's breast almost to my lips, my hand at her calf. Who knows what small anxiety will be furrowing my brow since I will still be thinking of myself as having taken Lillian's place. I will not yet know that Navaz has tickets home in the back of her wallet just as now Lillian does not know of the airline tickets concealed in the side pouch of my briefcase. Navaz will be weak from her illness and pleasures just taken. I will have overturned the courtesies of her sickbed, will have slipped from my bed to hers, will have drawn from her those moans and low cries which, days before, her fever induced in her. It will be the night when the houseboys couldn't sleep, next door's turn to be driven from their bed, to wait it out with cups of tea in the kitchen.

35

Navaz is well for a day. She has that kind of well-being only possible after a violent illness. Her body, which she is unaccustomed to thinking about, now feels peculiarly hers, like property. She does not say this exactly; that is, she does not say to me, 'I am unaccustomed to thinking about my body but today it feels strangely mine, as if it were my property.' Rather, she contemplates her body with a new enjoyment, we could almost say pride. She pushes her hair off her forehead, imitating the way my own hand had rested at her head when I checked her temperature, that sickroom gesture here reworked as stylish bravado, as a sign of rude health. Lying on the sand in front of the chalet, she studies her bare arm, turning it over and back as if it were not already hers but some covetable object. The memory of her body's recent treachery enlivens her. She pays a close attention to its mechanisms, the way the eyes move in their sockets, how the stomach is suspended in her torso between gullet and intestine. For twenty-four hours, her body performs without fault, like plant machinery on open day.

On Thursday morning when I wake, Navaz is reading the medical section of our travel guide. She is up to the chapter on hookworm and jigger fleas.

'Are you not well?' I avoid the word *sick*, which seems somehow impolite given the pleasure taken in her health only the previous day.

'I don't feel one hundred percent.' There is an edge of reserve to Navaz's voice, as if some critical distinction is being maintained between not being well and less than a hundred percent health. She looks well enough, perhaps a little flushed and bright-eyed. Her symptoms, it turns out, are nothing very specific: a slight queasiness, a head that aches when it is moved quickly, a dry mouth.

'I'd think nothing of it if it hadn't been for the day before yesterday.' Navaz is trying to set a light tone. She is not sure whether to get up or not: it feels like a strategic decision. I open the curtains. Navaz calls this view 'our beach aspect' because, although we are facing the sea, we can't see the water because of the trees along the beach road. Navaz reads me passages from our guidebook: *the female jigger flea burrows under the skin near the toes to lay her eggs.*

Two hours pass before it is clear that Navaz is sick again. She takes up where she left off, as if her being sick is a book or some knitting that she had cast aside for a moment. She lies back in our bed, her forehead one minute hot and dry to touch, the next, gleaming under a cool sweat. I collect the few blankets stored in the wardrobe and spread them over her, tucking the smooth edge of the sheet around her neck and chin. I fetch some ice cubes and run them around her chapped lips, along the lines of her collar bones. Navaz's head turns hot and cold under my anxious palm. She talks to me, to Lillian, of stories she has read or perhaps they are things that have happened to her. I think she sleeps for a while although she is so restless in the bed, twisting her head under my hand, that it is hard to say whether she is sleeping or simply feverish. Every half hour, she goes downstairs to the bathroom, holding the railing as if she were on a ship. The modesty of the closed bathroom door does not protect either of us from her groaning.

During one of these seclusions, I strip the sodden sheets from the bed and take them to reception for a fresh pair. The woman at the desk seems unhappy with me before she even hears my request.

'You and your friend have not left your rooms.' She is looking down at a piece of paper on her desk as if the movements of all her guests might be charted there. 'My girls cannot clean until you go down to the beach.' I show my damp armload over the top of the reception desk.

'My friend is sick,' I say, borrowing her idiom for ease of understanding. 'We will be needing clean sheets.'

'Would you like me to call for the doctor?' She manages to make this seem less an offer of assistance than a calling of my bluff. It is not that I don't have Navaz's best interests at heart but my first thought is that we don't want a doctor meddling in our affairs. Still,

I am not sure if I am doing the right things for Navaz, my remedies and comforts derived from some dimly remembered images of my mother tending me.

'Yes, we need the doctor,' I say to the woman who seems poised for action, her hand resting on the telephone. 'Clean sheets and the doctor.'

'He won't do house calls,' she says, handing over a pair of sheets without qualm, small price for such victory. 'My cousin can drive you to the doctor's surgery, no delay.'

Navaz is waiting upstairs, sitting on the edge of the unmade bed, wrapped in a blanket. She looks terrible, greasy and pale like bacon drippings. I do not ask how she is; she does not offer any information. I wonder what percentage she would rate herself now. As soon as the bottom sheet is on the bed, I lie her down, making the bed around her. Before the last blanket is tucked about her head, she gets up again, makes her way downstairs on unsteady shipboard legs. She does not close the door this time and from the top of the stairs I can see her sitting on the toilet, vomiting into a bucket held between her knees. For the first time I see her symptoms as evidence of her suffering, not signs of a new intimacy afforded me. It is a shaming moment. I can see it makes me look bad, this admission that I had reduced another's sickness to my benefit. I have always wanted to use this beautiful turn of phrase: *Let me explain.* While I had understood Navaz's fever, her shivering and sweating, her talking in her sleep, as proof that all was not as it should be, I had imagined that, given my unwavering attentions, these afflictions, like those paroxysms of sexual pleasure, were not entirely unpleasant in context. And being not altogether unpleasant for Navaz, they allowed me a less equivocal pleasure: a certain responsibility, a liberty, power.

Now, however, I see my miscalculation. I see Navaz in the bathroom, holding the bucket to her chest as if it were her most valued possession. I see how she would give up her body in a moment—that body she was so pleased with only yesterday—but that her body will not surrender her. Navaz is being reminded that she is flesh. Her body is so insistently detailing its materiality that there is no possibility of her misrecognising herself as anything else. Worse yet, she realises all this before I do and must leave the bathroom door open so that I might be infected by her knowledge. At the moment that I realise all the comforts I can offer Navaz are as dust, I hurry down the stairs towards her, my hands held out, my head tilted to one side, in a clumsy dramatisation of *comfort*. There is nothing in the bucket, only a translucent smear of jellied saliva running a line from Navaz's mouth to its plastic side, yet her stomach goes on retching as if it were a bad habit it can't quite shake. Navaz is crying. Perhaps the day before yesterday, or even this morning, I would have thought to myself that I had never seen her cry before, once more adding her symptoms to my storehouse of experiences. Now, seeing how Navaz is at the mercy of her body, or more simply, seeing how she *is* her body, I note only that she cries without effort, involuntarily, as she does everything else. Tears fall from Navaz's eyes as if her tear duct were just another aperture over which she has no control. I wash her face with a flannel, rinse it in the basin and apply it to the back of her neck until she can stop heaving over the bucket. Navaz walks upstairs, resting on each step. I swirl some water through the bucket, a useless gesture in the name of hygiene, and put it beside her bed.

I sit on the edge of the bed, take Navaz's hand in mine like someone about to deliver bad news.

'I am going to take you to a doctor,' I say. Navaz does not protest but she does not agree either. She is in exactly the same position when I return from reception having made the necessary arrangements, arms wide, knees curled, like those chalk outlines the police draw around victims. I slide her into some clothes—her head is too tender to have her hair brushed—and almost carry her down to the taxi that has pulled up at our door. Outside is another world: the beach makes everything seem easy and people are moving about slowly, eating and laughing in the sun. Even though he knows he is taking us to the doctor, the taxi driver seems determined not to spoil the holiday atmosphere. He wears his hair long and tells us where the best discos are. He calls them 'discothèques' with a touching respect.

'Do you like to dance?' he asks, looking over his shoulder so we can see ourselves reflected in his mirror sunglasses.

The doctor works from the back of his house. It seems so unlikely that a doctor will be waiting inside the plastered outhouse under the palms that I ask the driver if he is sure this is where the doctor lives. Inside, I examine the doctor's certificate hanging on the wall. Its seals and signatures are no comfort. It looks like the sort of thing you would put on the wall if you were pretending to be a doctor. At a desk the doctor sits, reading back copies of the *National Geographic*. He nods slowly when he sees Navaz come in as if she were a certain type that he could recognise from across the room, as if he had seen all this before.

'Your mouth is dry. You feel queasy.' The doctor speaks in the suggestive tones of a hypnotist. 'Your head is tender and aches when you move it.' Navaz does not offer a single symptom. She hangs her head over her knees and weeps as if some privacy of hers has been disclosed. The doctor is interested in what he calls 'purges'. He asks questions that cannot be answered.

'How many times?' Navaz raises her tearful face.

'How many times this morning?' I am not sure what to count. Episodes? In which case we might say twelve or fifteen. Or individual muscle contractions which would have our total in the hundreds?

'Continuous.' I say this word with conviction, as if it were specialist vocabulary, as if it had a particular precision to it.

'You will go to the laboratory at Margao,' says the doctor, writing something on a piece of paper. 'Your stool will be tested.' He hands me two sealed envelopes. 'Depending on the result of the examination, you will fill one of these scripts at the chemist. You will drink frequently and you will come back if you have not improved in five days.'

In the taxi, I steal a sidelong look at Navaz. Has she noticed the doctor's reference to 'five days'? We are supposed to return home tomorrow to coincide with a letter from Nishimura but Navaz is unconcerned. Her world is mapped by the limits of her skin. My own world is peculiarly circumscribed by Navaz's skin. I am constantly touching it under the pretext of medical attention. At the laboratory, I help Navaz from the car, one hand at the damp back of her neck. Navaz has lost weight in such a short time that it doesn't seem possible. Even her bones seem attracted to her skin: those usually secret supports of hips and ribs have risen to the surface, a reminder that the skin is, in effect, just a politeness. I am starting to mistake Navaz for her tears. She is damp and unshaped. I help her upstairs to our bed.

My memory of these days is as if I were the feverish one. There are other doctors, return trips to the medical laboratory, a hospital admission. Always, I am there at Navaz's side. It is me she looks for when she opens her eyes. She looks around her bed, half sitting up, pulling against the intravenous drip in her arm, until her eyes lock with mine. She has nothing to say to me. Once she knows that I am there, she lies down again, shuts her eyes. I understand perfectly, without a word. I am the representative of her body. In this strange space, I intercede for it. I engage the doctor in a discussion about the difference between amoebic and bacillary dysentery. In the hospital, I check that the sterile pack around the needle has not been tampered with before I allow the drip to be set up. I let Navaz sleep while I sign forms in her name. When she is able to travel again, I sign her discharge slip and take her to the airport with a piece of surgical tape over the puncture marks in her arm.

36

Professor Mody's first steps on the safari park are like a televised moonwalk. The bus door is shut behind him like an airlock. Everyone crams against the windows as before although some cordon of courtesy or fear keeps clear the space around my seat. I do not have to move into the window seat vacated by the professor for a better view: nobody jostles against me from the aisle; nobody obscures my line of sight. In his pale safari suit, Professor Mody is a tropical astronaut, his short sleeves exposing his arms to the radiation of alien suns. If he does not actually bob against gravity's absence, float across the heat-soaked plain, he does at least seem to move in slow motion. I see the frame-by-frame disarticulations of his legs and arms through the smeary, reinforced glass of my porthole as he illustrates the miracle of those ordinary motor functions *walk*, *turn* and *wave*.

His wave is breathtaking in its confidence. It is the wave of a public figure. His hand comes up to the level of his broad smile and makes several open-palmed wipes before him. It is not only the scale of the wave, its slow circuits of the unmoving air in front of the professor's face, that makes him seem as if he were a public figure. It is the way in which it is entirely remote from that everyday gesture of waving whose crude mechanisms it nevertheless imitates. The wave of the private individual is addressed to somebody. It is capable of different, even oppositional, inflections—*hello*, *goodbye*, *look at me*—but it is always addressed to somebody. The wave of the public figure, however, is not addressed to anyone, not even those members of the press and paparazzi who record its metronomic tick. It is performed in the round; it provides, in the language of the public figure, a photo opportunity. And what does it say, that self-absorbed wave that needs no address? Nothing but *I am waving, I am waving*.

Although no bank of cameras squeezes off multiple exposures

of the professor's foreshortened figure, he does not economise his gestural repertoire. His wave is fully elaborated; it turns through two hundred and seventy degrees with no lessening of intensity. As it sweeps the side of the bus—and it seems like the beam from a lighthouse, always focused but indifferent to what its passage might illuminate—a few of those less tightly packed against the glass lift their cameras to their faces as if by instinct. Again, it is only the man with the garland who actually takes a picture, winds the film along, takes another just to be sure. His garland is less jaunty than it was. It has twisted over his shoulder and hangs down his back like a leash. I try to imagine how he will caption his photographs when he makes up his holiday album, those high-angle shots of a man smiling in a dusty field, one arm caught at the limit of its wave. The professor's wave is making its return sweep. To his credit, he does not hesitate at my single face in the window. This is the man who has stood hours in the lane outside my apartment for a glimpse of that which he now passes over as if it held no interest for him. I had not thought him capable of such professionalism.

Now the professor stops waving and walks away from the bus, following the line of the road, as if he intends to leave the park on foot. The guide confers with the driver. It is impossible to understand what they are saying. The guide seems agitated. He shakes his keys at the door, at the window where the professor's purposeful back can be seen making down the track, over his shoulder, at the rest of the tour party. The driver is a model of self-restraint. He wags his head slowly from one side to the other to indicate that he sees the merit of every plan. It is the guide who leans forward and turns the key in the ignition. The driver jerks in his seat; the bus stalls, is restarted. In low gear, the bus follows the professor, soon drawing level with him. The guide opens the door but even the sound of it swinging back against the body of the bus does not make the professor turn his head. With the bus tracking at his shoulder, he continues to walk, head a little low, shoulders sloped, as if he proceeded with difficulty. He reminds me of Lillian, how she swung down the path in her rubber trousers, walking into the face of an invisible blizzard.

The professor is hamming it up now. He angles his head up

towards the bus and, from under the weight of one glowering eyebrow, gives me a wink. It is overblown and shamelessly theatrical: his eyelid rolls up and back like a pantomime curtain. He sets his face again, arms pumping in counterpoint to each step like a distance skater. What must he be thinking out there on his own, knowing for once that he has my attention, that I watch him while he mimes oblivion? I look along his sights, imagining that heat on my shoulderblades, the bus travelling at walking pace on my left hand. Up ahead, there is something yellow or brown against all that other yellow and brown but I know, almost before I see it, that this is a lion. I know that the professor has seen it too; that this is his joke, his wink.

Standing in the doorway, the guide seems not to have noticed what surely the driver sees through his double windscreen. He is only saying to Professor Mody, 'Please, sir, back on the bus. You are upsetting your lady friend.' He is making that up, of course. He would like me to be sobbing into some small handkerchief, I am sure, or shrilling at him in the doorway to do something, do something. I am not without feeling. Something moves inside me, something slides, something turns into something else. I understand that the professor is not doing this for me. He does it for himself in the desperate way that is possible when you imagine you have nothing to lose. The professor does not step down from the safari bus for me but he does it in front of me which is perhaps more touching. There is always something more to lose.

The lion is now too close to pass unnoticed. At this range, her coat is darker than the ground. She is the same colour as the patch of dirt visible in the shadow of her belly. There is no roaring, no knocking of cameras against the glass. A few heads turn to look at me but I am dull sport compared to the sight of the professor and the last steps marking the distance between him and the lion. The guide becomes frantic.

'A lion! A lion!' he calls, although it is impossible that the professor could have failed to see her. He leans from the door and grasps the professor by the shoulder, twisting him towards the bus but unable to make him board.

'Think of your family,' he begs. I am distracted for a moment by the incongruous thought of the professor's family. It occurs to me, in a more nuanced way than time seems to allow, that in those other rooms that I have never seen in Professor Mody's apartment he could have more than just servants; a wife, perhaps even children. The guide lowers his voice as the professor approaches the lion. His last words are almost whispered through the crack of the closing door, 'You asked me to let you out.'

The professor does not break his stride as he walks up to the lion. He takes up a position directly behind her, standing so close that the hairs along her spine can be differentiated against the backdrop of his trousers. In his safari suit, he is well costumed. He puts one hand to his hip and, shielding his eyes from the sun, looks away to the horizon. Or rather he would look to the horizon, if his view were not blocked by the side of the bus. If only he had one booted foot resting on the lion's chest, it would be a trophy photograph. No one thinks to take pictures this time. Professor Mody strikes a couple of poses—both hands on hips; reclining on one elbow, his feet at the lion's head, his head falling short of where her tail ends—before touching the lion. He puts his hand where her belly folds into the flank. His hand rises and falls with her breath. She opens an eye, throws her tail. From inside the bus, even with the door closed, her tail sounds like a length of rope hitting a deck. The professor stands, steps over her body, his shadow marking the place where his hand had rested. He climbs back on to the bus.

'You were right,' he says to the guide. 'They're as healthy as could be.'

No one speaks. We drive from the park as from the horrible scene of an accident.

37

I have to stop writing Nishimura's novel. It is a sad knowledge which I pretend not to have, like that other knowledge I had of Navaz's departure. For two weeks I knew she was leaving; I had looked in the back of her wallet, seen the date on her ticket. Yet, on the verge of departure, she seemed no less with me than before. She looked the same, displaced the same amount of air. That is, at least, what I said to myself: *she is no less with me than before.* Yet I looked at Navaz differently, knowing how these unassuming actions—these raisings of cutlery to her mouth, these sleepings and wakings—were only rehearsals for a life that was being held open for her elsewhere. I looked at her, a thumb to her eyebrow, her cigarette pointed at the ceiling, one hand catching at her dressing gown just below the collarbone, not as if I memorised, but as if I were remembering, her. She was, for me, already in the past tense. I made no attempt to imprint myself with the dent of her temple, the way her dressing gown fell against her skin. An apparition, already a ghost of herself, I said only, *Remember how she held her cigarette* and *Navaz used to shake her hair back like that.* Then she was gone and I thought I would rather be dead than without her. There is no other, more credible, way of saying this.

I have to stop writing Nishimura's novel. I have no idea how long it is, just a sense that it is running down. Sanki, Beatrice and Mr Oliver have been circling each other like dogs on heat and even one more cycle may make them seem plastic, as unconvincing as horses on a carousel. Even at this stage, when I can see it cannot continue, I don't know how the novel will end. What I know, instead, is how I will end with its last line, how there will be no possible stay of that conclusion. It seems there is always something more to lose. For some time, I have been thinking that I will simply stop; that Navaz will have to conclude that the novel is finished, as I once had to, when no more arrives. But the time for that abruptness, that amputative end with no denouement, has passed. It was Nishimura's final line and I have written myself beyond that strategy. I entertain several possibilities: a secret liaison, a chance discovery, accusations and tearful recriminations. Still, the faces in these scenes remain uncertain or, rather, they take each other's place as if they were trying out for a part. One night I woke with the whole thing complete in my head. I would expand the role of Roger, the undistinguished boy with the soiled shirt, and he would take up with Beatrice, maybe even take her away, certainly remove her from the reach of Sanki and Mr Oliver. It was morning before I saw the uselessness of my plan. There was, of course, no opportunity to rewrite what I had already committed to the post: I could only continue, there was no going back.

I sit at my typewriter as if at a piano. I have given myself two days. When I lift my elbows off the felted green of the card table, my hands shake. I had imagined that I would have to think of yet some other scenario where the three of them might be drawn together or apart. My rote-learned vocabulary lists—they come back to me sleeping: *butcher, bank, drygoods store, millinery; bread, milk, tea*—seemed to make a shopping expedition inevitable although I could see how unlikely it would be for Mr Oliver to accompany his maid and his boarder to town. Reading over my drafts of the last page I had sent to Navaz, however, I realised that this would not be necessary. Just because time has elapsed here, just because the professor has visited and left in a borrowed shirt, is no reason to make parallel shifts in the novel. For Sanki, Mr Oliver and Beatrice, bent over the table in the darkening dining room, only a few minutes have passed. Upstairs Roger has just consigned his shirt to the pile of clothes in the corner of his room or hung it over the back of his chair, good for one more day. I have lost interest in Roger: we never know the fate of his shirt or even see him again. He has vanished as surely as if he had an airline ticket in the back of his wallet.

Mr Oliver sits at the head of the table: Sanki sits at his left hand, Beatrice at his right. Sanki adds up the columns of figures under their initials. Beatrice has won: there was never any doubt of that. A strange inertia grips them. Surely it is too dark for them to sit any longer? My atmospheric lighting is being turned down like a gas lamp. Soon they will be ridiculous figures, sitting in the dark, no longer able to make out each other's faces across the width of the table. Yet it does not seem at all obvious where else they might go. Sanki stands at last. He is like a man who dreams that he is to give a public address but once on his feet before the crowd realises he has left his notes at home, that he has forgotten what he was asked to speak about, that he is naked. He says that he is going to give the garden a soaking. Perhaps Beatrice will follow him out to the vegetable garden and something else will grow under the green promise of the hose. Beatrice, as if remembering the view the back window affords, gathers together their cups and saucers and withdraws to the kitchen.

Mr Oliver stands. He hooks his hand through the bend of Sanki's arm but there is no need. Already Sanki is moving, not to the back door and the rustling garden beyond, but further into the house, through the dining room door, to the bottom of the main staircase. And if it seems that Mr Oliver is leading Sanki, if it seems that the older man has the younger by the arm and is tugging him upstairs, gently but firmly, as one pulls a wide-eyed needle through some stout fabric, then it is only for show. For Sanki is climbing the stairs of his own accord: like yeast, like hope, he rises. On the first floor, he passes his own open door, makes no attempt to climb the last few stairs to Mr Oliver's room. Now he is slightly ahead of Mr Oliver, who still has him by the arm. He leads him to the end of the corridor, to the room that is not used by anyone. The boys call it the music room but they take that on trust for there is no dusty or cloth-covered piano, not even a music stand, to hint at its remembered function.

Downstairs, Beatrice is singing. She imagines herself at the centre of a small world. No, she imagines herself a small-world divinity whose next word, whose next action, shapes, changes, has power. No one pays her any attention but she is singing, stretching her head back, her voice being pulled from her throat like entrails. Her voice has a kind of lie in it, a kind of quaver or, as she says to herself, still savouring the almost electric charge of words, a tremolant. She pitches her voice to carry over the susurrous spray of water, the hose held in Sanki's hand as he contrives to look over his shoulder at her head moving in the orange square of the kitchen window, her throat gleaming white and smooth behind the glass. She cannot see Mr Oliver in the darkness of the dining room—nor will she be caught looking—but she knows how he will have his head in his hands, not despairing but trying to keep his anticipation, which even now creeps to the kitchen and rubs against Beatrice's ankle, between himself and the dark brown top of the refectory table. It is for Mr Oliver that Beatrice takes care to articulate the words of her song. Sanki will only catch the tune, and perhaps even that imperfectly, but Beatrice's careful words slide into Mr Oliver's ear as if oiled. *My baby thinks she's a train*, she sings, taking trouble over the s sounds. I am not able to make Beatrice ungrammatical so Lillian's song sounds more formal in her mouth: *she does not know the difference between pleasure and pain.*

In the upstairs doorway, the maid's voice is like static. Unwatched, she is a maid again. Sanki takes Mr Oliver in his arms. Perhaps it would be more accurate to say that he takes Mr Oliver's arms. He holds the arms above the elbow and presses them against Mr Oliver's sides. Sanki is shorter than Mr Oliver and must tiptoe when he kisses him. Sanki is not so interested in kissing Mr Oliver but he is working under a logic that tells him if he is allowed to do this much then he will not be prevented from doing those other things for which he has more of a taste. He slides his tongue under Mr Oliver's as carefully as if it were a thermometer. They move into the music room. The door is closed behind them. 'Time,' says Sanki to Mr Oliver, 'weighs heavy on my hands.' Their clothes come off easily enough because there is a vocabulary for it: *jacket, vest, waistcoat, trousers, shirt, socks, pants, shoes.* Sanki takes off his underpants last. They slide down like a flag. Mr Oliver sits naked on the windowsill, one leg over the other, wrestling with his Oxford shoes.

There is an awkward moment as words fail me. I know *hands, feet, face, arms, legs* but Sanki and Mr Oliver are revealing parts of the body I cannot name. What is the word for armpit, for testicle, for belly button? Sanki turns Mr Oliver to face the window, one hand moves down the front of Mr Oliver's body, the other takes hold of his own penis or *staff of love*, as I have cribbed from Yukio. Mr Oliver's back is broad enough that Sanki almost thinks he is lying in bed. He seems more solid than the window frame against which he leans for support. The maid's voice comes to them as if through the floorboards, *she does not know the difference between pleasure and pain.* Mr Oliver's face pushes against the glass. His cheek slides across the gathering condensation. Below the window, the unwatered garden is a dark patch against the lawn. Beatrice stands silent in the kitchen. The table is wiped, the chairs put up for the night; she will choose the one who is least like her.

38

Back at the city bus terminal, I do not care to say goodbye to Professor Mody. On the return trip, he has ridden beside me like an angel, silent, almost luminous. The bus stops at Juhu Beach but we do not get down. There are crowds trampling the sand. Through the window I can see people target-shooting at balloons, riding horses and camels, throwing hoops over bars of soap: they look like the background to a painting of the professor. In the city again, there seems more to be had from the day. It is early yet, just gone five, but I ask the professor to have dinner with me. I have in mind something grand, a private room somewhere, but lose confidence at the last moment, suggesting only a Chinese restaurant I have seen on the street between the professor's apartment and mine. Navaz's family once recommended it to us which makes me think it will have an unadventurous menu and be full of families who pay us too much attention.

At five-thirty, the restaurant is empty. I angle for a corner table, my earlier wish for a private room reinstalling itself more modestly as a desire to be partially obscured from sight. The manager approaches. He slips the menu on to the table as if it were a bribe.

'Something to drink, sir?' The professor waves his hand at me across the table.

'Madam, something to drink?' I had not thought to have a drink but the idea is attractive. The bottles of beer that the professor and I used to share at his apartment seem suddenly to be weighed about with a symbolism I wish to inflect this evening's meal.

'Perhaps a beer,' I say, giving the professor a glance that, if he had been looking, would have been read as 'significant'.

'Golden Eagle, Rosy Pelican, Cannon Extra Strong, Punjab, Kingfisher, Guru.' The manager lists these brands from memory. None of their names sound familiar to me from those evenings at Professor Mody's. It occurs to me then that, even if I get the beer right, I am calling on something dated, something which speaks of an expectant companionship that has just been exceeded.

'Whisky?' I have the professor's attention now. His head swings around from the window as if he has been called, as if 'whisky' is his name.

'Whisky, yes madam. Indian-made foreign whisky.'

The whisky is served in large tumblers, no ice. There is surely more whisky in each glass than ought to be drunk in polite company. I am not, as you have guessed, a whisky drinker. When I raise the glass to my lips, the fumes skin the inside of my nose, fill my mouth as if I had already taken a sip. Across the table, Professor Mody's eyes are watering. I have things to tell him; he sits opposite me, a tear forming in the corner of his right eye. Inferior sentences form in my head—*you were magnificent today*—but I do not rise to their bait. The manager passes the table several times before closing in for our order. Professor Mody is having chicken in black bean sauce. I ask after the more plainly titled 'Roast Pork'.

'How does the roast pork come?' The manager seems not to understand my question.

'Roast pork.' He runs his finger underneath the words on the menu, looking to see that I follow his direction. 'Roast pork.'

'But how does it come?' I ask.

'It comes like roast pork,' says the manager. 'It is like bacon.'

A sentence which does not have 'roast pork' in it comes into my mind. It is my sentence for the professor.

'I will take it,' I say to the manager, who bows himself away from our table.

'Today I looked at you . . .' I am addressing the professor now: a shiver or, it can be better said in French, a *frisson* runs under and across the table, knitting me up with Professor Mody as I admit having looked at him, having arranged him before me as perhaps even now the roast pork is being arranged for me on a plate in the kitchen. The manager is back at my side.

'It is like ham,' he says. I wave him from me like a fly.

'Today I looked at you and saw that you had the mark of the chosen about you.' That look has not left the professor. Even now he appears like a religious statue about to bleed or weep. Out of the corner of my eye, I see the dark column of the manager advance on the table. He is up on his toes and the hunch of his creeping shoulders, the low, almost confidential, tone of his voice, signal his desire not to interrupt.

'It is like a pig.' He shrugs his shoulders as if it were an obscenity from which he could not protect me.

'I will have it.' I speak out of the corner of my mouth, without turning my head. The manager falls away from the table like a scab.

I seem to be short on words. It is as if the last passage of Nishimura's novel has drained them from me. I imitate the professor's gesture when he is stuck for words in translation: I hold my mouth open and cock my head to one side. The professor has the boundless patience of a holy relic. He prompts me, draws testimony from me with the comforting efficiency of a poultice.

'The mark of the chosen?' It is not quite a question but, like the piece of fencing held open this afternoon at the safari park, it has an inviting lift to it.

'I hadn't seen it before,' I say dully, as if it were some ordinary something, a birthmark or a tattoo. Our meals arrive. The professor bends a prayerful head over his plate. Later, the manager brings our bill on a saucer with two fortune cookies. My fortune reads, *You have an unusual equipment for success*; the professor's cookie is empty. I pay for our meal.

On the street, I am drunk. It seems barely possible given that I can see, through the restaurant window, my glass with two centimetres of whisky still in it. The street lamps are smeared against the sky and I move around on the pavement to disguise my unsteadiness.

'I have something to post.' The professor raises his eyebrows at me. Clearly this is not the turn either of us has been expecting.

'I will walk you.' The professor's gallantry does not have him say, *I will walk with you*, but *I will walk you*. I feel myself trot beside him like a dog. We pass the professor's apartment on the way to the post office. His light is on. Someone is expecting him home. We avert our eyes and hurry by, colluding with each other in some meaningless chat. I pull out my last letter to Navaz and, as if it were any other letter, drop it through the after-hours mailbox. How can it be that my bag feels heavier after the envelope has fallen through the slot?

My letters to Navaz always seemed to hold open a passage between us, a passage which did not depend on her realising who had written them or even the certain knowledge that they had been received. While I was writing to her, I had no need for the reassurance of flight timetables. Airmail suggests absence but I allowed those cool blue envelopes to lure me into thinking that they more ably demonstrated absence overcome. Those letters, posted every third day, marked a trajectory that I might at any point follow. As long as I did not put them to the test, they offered me the promise of Hansel and Gretel's crumbs, a safe return. Knowing that the envelope which has just this moment passed from my fingers is the last possible letter leaves me stranded. Even before I let it drop through the slot, it wants nothing more to do with me. It seems final and irrevocable like a heat-seeking missile whose pre-programmed focus on its destination allows no comfort for its source.

It takes twice as long to regain the professor's apartment. I am hoping he will offer to walk me home but instead he invites me up.

'Will you come up?' he asks, his hand gesturing at the lighted window which I think now he may well have arranged this morning before he met me. I see immediately how this thwarting of my plans might realise them. There had always been problems with my own apartment. The card table is barely up to the weight of the typewriter and some elegant nostalgia prohibits my imagining the professor stretched on either of the single beds.

'Certainly,' I say and then, before I lose heart, 'I will make your back.' The professor makes no remark. Or rather, pretending to make no remark, he walks in front of me across the road towards his apartment, unlocks the door and precedes me up the stairs, displaying at all times to best advantage that back which I have presumed to make.

Upstairs, all is as I remember it. Professor Mody does not embarrass either of us with protracted negotiations. He stands by the couch and removes his clothes, a simpler vocabulary of slip-on shoes, the two pieces of his safari suit, generous white underpants. He has the grace to hesitate before removing these last. They slide from his reluctant legs. I, also, do not allow myself to panic. I attend to the professor as to a difficult equation. He seems to be hovering at one end of the couch but already I can see the difficulty its armrests pose. I arrange some cushions on the rug and the professor lies across these as if trained. I kneel beside him, then straddle his buttocks, thinking I may as well, as my mother was fond of saying, be hung for a sheep as a lamb. Professor Mody does not know the saying: he lies quiet and meek beneath me. I tip my bag on to the floor and, from the debris of the day, take up a bottle of moisturiser.

Remembering the style of the masseuse, I begin at the base of the professor's head, work the skin at the back of his neck, let his spine lead me down his back. The cream, almost colourless on my hands, leaves a white film on the professor. As soon as it has been absorbed by his skin, I move on. Finally I am sitting on the crook of his knees, my hands kneading his buttocks. There is nothing firm to them; they give under my hands as if they were without a muscle. One of my hands continues to squeeze the professor, the other drops to my side, gropes the spilled contents of my bag until it finds one of the batons we were given at the milk colony. The baton is light, half the width of my wrist and rests in my hand with an intent which seems at odds with its red lettering. I run it back and forth between the professor's buttocks until it catches at the only muscle the professor has to offer. The professor has brought one knee up under his belly at the baton's instruction. The moment when I see it take reminds me how the snake-charmer's flute caught against the snake, puckering its skin. It hardly seems the same day. Soon it is no longer possible to read *Aarey Milk*. There is no chance that I might mistake this body under my hand for Navaz's. Professor Mody's watery buttocks are so distracting I cannot even think of her. It is not that I put her to the back of my mind but that, baton in hand, I cannot recall her. My last letter is shrinking away from me, becoming smaller and smaller as it falls towards Navaz. Here it is going on for midnight: I do not know what time it is in that other country. *Creamy! Dreamy!*